GRACE LIKE SNOW

*Essays from
the Heartland*

Gayle Larson Schuck

All scripture references are from the New International Version Bible unless otherwise noted.

ISBN: 978-1-7372571-1-0

Cover photo by Andra Marquardt
Author photo by Miranda Stanley
Essays on Life section photo: Larry Schuck snowblowing a path to the back door.
Personal Essay section photo: Grandsons at Missouri River beach.
Holidays section photo: A long-ago Christmas filled with toys and a tinseled tree.
The Writer section photo: Gayle at an impromptu book signing.
Faith section photo: Trinity Lutheran Church, Litchville, N.D.

Acknowledgements

Writing is a solitary job. First, breathing space is needed for the creative juices to flow. When inspiration comes, the writer then falls into a bottomless pit as she tries to find just the right way to phrase a thought. Next, she exposes her perfect prose to a small audience, and wonders if they will like her new creation.

All of this time, she tells herself she is not interested in publishing anything. Ever. Again. This is followed by taking steps to begin the lengthy, anxiety-producing process of publishing.

When at last her work is published, she knows she cannot take much of the credit because lots of people have had a part in bringing her to the day when a box of books lands on her doorstep.

I am indebted to the following people and so many more. So, thank you to:

My husband, Larry. Thanks for being my most devoted fan, front-line proof-reader, and for willingly driving me to speaking engagements and book signings. It would be a lonely life without you.

The Wordsmiths writers group. Although we write in many genres our group works. Thank you for bringing your unique talents to the group. Your honesty and encouragement are appreciated and valued.

My family. My sons, who find my occupation something of a mystery but support me anyway. To my daughter-in-law who has faithfully proofed all of my books. And to my grandsons who share a love of writing.

My writing friends and mentors across the nation. What a joy it is to have someone to hash out concerns about everything from commas to how your books should be classified.

Everyone who has ever sponsored a writers conference. Having attended conferences across the country, you have long had an influence on my writing.

Faithful friends and devoted readers. You'll never know how much your encouragement fuels my writing.

The Lord Jesus, who changed my heart and gave me a new life so many years ago, and who still inspires me today.

Contents

Introduction

As a writer, an ever-flowing river of words course through my mind. The words come in the dawn or while riding in the car or hiking a dirt path through the woods. Sometimes they actually make it onto paper. And sometimes I actually type them into the computer.

My computer stores hundreds of stories and essays. Sometimes they are actually published. You'll find them in my four novels or as one of the 75 blog posts published on www.gaylelarsonschuck.com.

This book includes essays published as blog posts between 2015 to 2022. Most of the messages are timeless, but some of them reflect the year in which they were written. My apologies to the reader if that causes any confusion.

In addition, a number of unpublished stories are included in this book. Some of these are quite personal.

The book is divided into five topical sections. They include essays on life in general and personal essays. The other three sections are on writing, holidays and faith.

If these essays stir up your memories, I hope you will write down those aha moments in life, those cherished time, and your own thoughts on faith, holidays and even world events.

Essays on Life

Light from the Prairie

The Prairie Lighthouse blog is inspired by coastline lighthouses, beacons of light to all who travel the oceans. In much the same way, churches stand like lighthouses in an ocean of prairie, pointing the way to God.

This blog is a place to find faith, hope and courage today. I am a prairie girl, inspired by rolling hills that stretch to the horizons, just as the waves of the ocean tilt and roll, offering endless shades of light and texture. My daily place of inspiration is my own backyard, where birds, squirrels, chukars, and an occasional wild turkey or mallard delight the soul. Blue spruce, bull pines, a red maple, a white birch and a Mountain ash are visible from my office window.

The trees in my website banner are ancient cottonwoods rooted along the Missouri River shores 40 miles north of Bismarck. It is likely Lewis and Clark walked beneath those very trees in 1804-06. This prairie girl loves to spend time near the Missouri, a powerful body of water that cuts through the heartland. There is nothing like feeling its sugar-fine sand between your toes.

Each morning I get an attitude adjustment from the comic section of the newspaper where *Sally Forth, Baby Blues, Pickles* and *Crankshaft* mirror my own daily crises. Sometimes the simple things in life, like the comics, are the most profound.

Peanuts is my all-time favorite cartoon. Charles Schultz aspired to be an artist as a teenager, but the high school yearbook rejected his artwork. He decided to take an art correspondence course instead. Then, he went on to produce *Peanuts* for 50 years. Schultz remained a common person in spite of his fame. He built an ice rink next to the Charles M. Schultz Museum in Santa Rosa, California. Sometimes he slipped in to watch the skaters or to take the Zamboni for a ride. Aren't we lucky he didn't give up his dream of becoming an artist because of the high school rejection?

I am a prairie girl, and I look forward to quiet times when God can speak to my heart. It is possible to sit on a quiet prairie hilltop and see everything in a 50-mile radius. It is possible to hear the whispers of God in water that laps a river's shore. The lazy hum of a bee on a flower on a hot summer day may encourage and nourish my soul.

At the end of the day, the Bible is my book of choice. My blue-covered copy is underlined, filled with scraps of paper and showing signs of hinge fatigue. Each underlined verse is an "a-ha" moment that makes me want to seize the nearest person and say, "Look at this!"

From Genesis through Revelation, the Bible tells the story of human failure and God's plan for redemption. It's the story of my redemption, too. That's why the Prairie Lighthouse blog will often include scripture.

Various topics that are on my mind will find a place here. This prairie girl has been around a few years and I hope my experiences and insights will have a positive impact on your life. I'm eager to talk about what it's like to be a first-time author (thrilling, hard) and also why I'm excited about my upcoming book.

*"And hope does not disappoint us, because
God has poured out his love into our hearts
by the Holy Spirit, whom he has given us."*
Romans 5:5 (NIV)

Today While the Blossoms Still Cling to the Vine

The other morning I awoke with a melody running through my mind. Though I couldn't remember the title or the words, it seemed like a good idea to pay attention to the jukebox in my head. Often the songs playing there offer insight into my emotions or current events.

Today, when I turned on the music channel, that very melody was playing. "Today" by the New Christy Minstrels came out in 1964. When I listened to the song, I knew there was a blog post in that five letter word "Today."

Today while the blossoms still cling to the vine I'll taste your strawberries, I'll drink your sweet wine. A million tomorrows shall all pass away Ere I forget all the joy that is mine today.

As I write this in my senior years, I recall writing an essay on "Yesterday" when I was a senior in high school. Now, I wonder how much a teenager could have to say about yesterday? I kept the paper, which is filled with jaded teenage wisdom. Although it couldn't have been too bad. When I met up with my English teacher decades later to thank him for encouraging me to write, I found he had also kept the essay.

Paradoxically, now that I have many yesterdays to write about, I'm writing about today. Because, really, today is what is important.

I can't be contented with yesterday's glory I can't live on promises winter to spring (winter to spring.)

So, besides humming this sweet ballad, how can we treasure today?

Take time to enjoy music or art, spend time with a friend, go for a walk. My very Norwegian Aunt Ianca Larson often commented, "The hurrier I go, the behinder I get." Getting away from our tasks or problems puts them in perspective. Ianca also liked to say, "Too soon old, too late smart." Let's be smart and make some guilt-free happy time.

"Worry is the interest paid by those who borrow trouble." George Washington said that, and he had plenty to worry about. We can make the most of each day by following his advice and that found in Matthew 6:34, "So do not worry about tomorrow; for tomorrow will care for itself. Each day has enough trouble of its own."

Begin each day by thanking God. There is a scene in the movie "The Orphan Train" where a room full of homeless orphans found much for which to be grateful. By comparison, my list of blessings is endless! There is a bonus in thanking and praising God, because it brings us into His presence; there is no more lovely place to be.

Encourage someone. Courage is the root word of both encourage and discourage. St. Paul, in I Thessalonians said, "Therefore encourage one another and build each other up..."

We all have a God-given call to be part of His family and be His representatives here on earth. Nothing makes today more rewarding than being in that sweet spot where we are making a difference. Need direction? Ask and then listen for His quiet voice in your heart.

Today is my moment and now is my story
I'll laugh and I'll cry and I'll sing. A million
tomorrows shall all pass away Ere I forget all
the joy that is mine today.

The Statue of Liberty

We're on a ferry that will stop at the Statue of Liberty and then drop us off at Ellis Island. The whole ferry is crowded, but we've managed to get seats on the top deck in the open air. We make a wide approach to the statue.

Behind me a man cries out, "Thee Stay-too uf Lee-bur-tee!" Over and over he shouts the words above the many languages being spoken around us. "Thee Stay-too uf Lee-bur-tee!" "Thee Stay-too uf Lee-bur-tee!"

Security at the Statue of Liberty remains high because of terror threats. So I wonder, is the guy behind me happy with or angry at America? Then he climbs up to stand on the bench. His bright blue shoes all but touch my backside.

"Thee Stay-too uf Lee-bur-tee! *What a be-a-u-tee-foll sight!*" The emotion in his voice is as deep as the harbor.

I look around to find a young dark-haired man attached to the blue shoes. A woman and a couple children crowd near him. His face shines, his arms are thrown wide. He clearly loves what the statue represents.

A minute later, the ferry docks at Liberty Island. I stand up and smile at the man and ask where he is from.

"Albania."

What I know about Albania can be written in a few words: Centuries of war, domination by dictators, under communism for decades.

The statue is a symbol of hope all around the world. So many people have endured tyranny since the Statue of Liberty was unveiled in 1886. I imagine them huddled in their dark abodes dreaming of life in the land of the freedom.

What did my ancestors think when they saw the American coastline for the first time? Did their hopes and dreams dare to spill out? Did they shout aloud? Did they stand on a bench and open their arms to their new country?

Compared to the man from Albania, my own patriotism is so...tepid. Oh how much we take for granted.

"The New Colossus" by Emma Lazarus is inscribed on the statue. Here are the words:

Not like the brazen giant of Greek fame,
With conquering limbs astride from land to
land;
Here at our sea-washed, sunset gates shall
stand
A mighty woman with a torch, whose flame
Is the imprisoned lightning, and her name
Mother of Exiles. From her beacon-hand
Glows world-wide welcome; her mild eyes
command
The air-bridged harbor that twin cities frame.

"Keep, ancient lands, your storied pomp!" cries
she
With silent lips. "Give me your tired, your poor,
Your huddled masses yearning to breathe
free,
The wretched refuse of your teeming shore.
Send these, the homeless, tempest-tost to me,
I lift my lamp beside the golden door!"

The Beginning

Sometimes what we think is the end is really the beginning.

We have a friend who is an auctioneer. He does a lot of farm auctions, which almost always happen because a farmer has financial or health problems. I asked our friend one day how he could bear to participate in these sad endings. His response surprised me. He said the auction released the farmer to get on with his life. Some go on to new careers, others can relax after a lifetime of toil. He didn't see the auction as an ending, but a new beginning. And so it is.

Larry and I experienced that many years ago. We left farming, a way of life that our families had lived for generations. For years, when we went back home, we could see how we would have fit into the community. Our sons would have grown up with the children of our friends. Our family would have been close by.

Still, leaving the farm allowed us both to go to college and have careers, with the bonus of weekends off and paid vacations. We made new lifelong friends and have other family living nearby. We've missed living in our hometown, but we haven't missed hailed crops, cattle lost to blizzards or the other hazards of farming. What appeared to be the end, was really only a new beginning.

We weren't the first to leave home in search of a better life. Our families came to America from Scotland, Norway, Bohemia and Germany, via Ukraine. Why did they leave their families and their countries? Most were forced by circumstances to try a new life. The truth is, most of us resist change and fear the unknown instead of embracing it.

A long time ago a group of people found a leader they truly loved. Their hopes were high! He would usher in a better life. Then a horrible thing happened. The leader was captured by his enemies and publicly executed. His followers were heartbroken at the turn of events and thought the end of everything had come. But it wasn't the end; it was really the beginning. Three days later Jesus rose from the grave!

Often a bad turn of events is really something that God makes into a new beginning. Death is that way. We cling to life, yet when it slips away from us, the Bible promises us a way to spend eternity in a place with no more tears or sighing. Jesus himself said he would go and prepare a place for us.

The beginning always comes after the end. The end of pregnancy brings birth. The end of childhood brings adult privileges and responsibilities. The end of a career brings opportunities to do those things that have been waiting.

Yes, the end is always the beginning. Knowing that fortifies us for the next phase of life. We don't need to take that next step alone. With quietness and confidence we can trust the Lord with our future. It is He who says he has a plan for our lives, and who gives us hope and a future.

Talking to Myself:
This Better be Good

Do you talk to yourself? Go on, admit it. We all do. Just last week my husband caught me saying to myself, "First, pick the weeds, and *then* play in the garden." I need to instruct myself or I'd never finish a project!

Our self-talk better be good, too, because it has a lasting impact on our hearts, minds and bodies. The power of words is a key to a life.

Think how hateful, mean-spirited words can hurt us. This morning in a television interview, a woman recalled her mother saying, "You'll never amount to anything." She believed those words and because of them, she took a path that led to destruction. In the same way, a little praise and encouragement can inspire us to do more, do better, be quicker and smile more.

If comments from others can have life-changing consequences, think of how our own self-talk affects us. Certainly, our own words have a big impact, because our internal chatter goes on all day, every day. Those internal thoughts become words. What comes out of our mouth is heard by our body's in-tegrated system, setting off complex chemical and neurological changes in our body, mind and spirit.

In his book, "Power in the Promises" Nick Harrison states, "During any given day, we all engage in some sort of self-talk. But too often our self-talk is along the lines of, 'I'm unhappy,' "I can't do this,'

I hate my life,' 'My marriage is shaky...'"

Isn't that the truth? And after we say, "I'm unhappy," we probably tell someone we are unhappy. Maybe we get a headache about that time or the old fibromyalgia springs up. Maybe we pick an argument, because by now we're also in a bad mood.

Our self-talk is important to our outlook. Harrison points out that there isn't such a thing as a trouble-free life, but we can learn to be happy in spite of our circumstances. The apostle Paul wrote, "I can do all things through Christ, who strengthens me." (Philippians 4: 13) Paul knew how to encourage himself and others, even though he was in prison when he wrote those words.

One of the best ways to season our self-talk with words of hope and lightness is to have a resource filled with inspiration. The best-selling book of all time, the Bible, is full of promises. And just to make it easier to find them, Harrison's book includes 100 biblical promises!

Here are few promises to think on, say aloud and savor for the coming week:

> *"For I know the plans I have for you,"*
> *declares the Lord, "plans to prosper you and*
> *not to harm you, plans to give you hope and*
> *a future." Proverbs 29:11*

> *"Come to me, all you who are weary and*
> *burdened, and I will give you rest." Matthew*
> *11:28*

> *"God shall supply all your needs according*
> *to His riches in glory by Christ Jesus."*
> *Philippians 4:19*

Don't Let the Sun Catch You Crying

In *By the Banks of Cottonwood Creek* the main character, Kelly Jorgenson said this: "Why are the most bitter and the most sweet tangled together?"

That's how I feel about sunshine. Summer is upon us and this prairie girl wants to play outside, whether it's having a cup of coffee on the front step in the morning sun or hiking along a trail in some place more adventuresome. However, like a two-edged razor, the sun has two sides. The life-giving force that allows our existence on planet earth can also cause skin cancer.

One in five Americans will develop skin cancer sometime in their lifetime, according to the American Academy of Dermatology. Over 2 million people will be diagnosed with skin cancer in 2015.

Until the second half of the twentieth century, people had the good sense to cover their skin. They wore hats, long pants and long-sleeved tops. Then tanning became popular. Is it any wonder that from 1973 to 2009 melanoma increased in men by 61% and doubled in women?

Growing up, I expected to get a good sunburn at the beginning of summer. After that, my northern European skin would tan a little. One year we went to the 100th anniversary of the Battle of Whitestone Hill. My mother and I both came away from that hot, cloudless day absolutely fried.

Mom later had skin cancer. So did all of her brothers, my three brothers, two sisters, and several nieces and nephews. This is serious, folks. A year ago last winter, my nephew died of melanoma. He was only 53.

My first round with cancer was on my neck many years ago. I went to a dermatologist to have a skin tag removed because it was irritated by clothing. It turned out to be squamous cell cancer.

A few years ago, a spot on my face began to grow bigger and darker. People began to politely suggest I have a doctor look at it, so I made an appointment. I spent two winters in treatment for a precancerous condition. The spot mostly disappeared after that, but now it's back. My dermatologist believes it's just pigmentation, but I have regular checkups.

There is much to say about causes and prevention of skin cancer. But right now, at the beginning of summer when the sun is so appealing and so strong, do this:

Every day, protect yourself and your children. Guys, this goes for you, too.

Wear a hat and long sleeves.

Avoid situations where you might get burned.

Use sunscreen on your face, neck, arms and legs, but don't totally rely on it.

For more information, check out the American Academy of Dermatology website at www.aad.org.

Be wise! Don't let the sun catch you crying because you've allowed it too much power in your life. The Bible states that

> *"If any of you lacks wisdom, he should ask*
> *God, who gives generously to all without*
> *finding fault, and it will be given to him."*
> *James 1:1*

Summer in Full Bloom

Summer is in full bloom here in the heartland. The daisies have outdone themselves. We've picked the first ripe tomatoes. The waist-high fields of soft yellow clover look like something painted by Monet. They give off a sweet scent that erases every negative thought about living in the far north. Life is good!

When summer is short, as it is here, you must take advantage of every fair day. Our friends invited us for a joyride in their Mustang convertible the other evening. We cruised past those clover fields and cut through the river bottoms to spend some time on the shore of the Missouri River.

We also go to the ballpark each week to watch the Blue Jays play. There is no better entertainment than watching pint-sized boys learning the game, their huge one-size-fits all shirts tucked artlessly into their pants.

They are all in the same ballpark, so to speak, just learning the game. Yes, you must touch one base before going to another. If you actually catch the ball, the batter is automatically out, so don't throw it to first base. It's also good to know that sometimes when you are running the bases, the voices shouting, "Go! Go!" belong to the other team.

It's hilarious fun watching their enthusiastic play. Their coach is persistent and patient. The onlookers cheer for each boy's success. The boys' skill grows with each game.

Oh, the optimism of youth who dream of making

a homerun! They are so willing to take a chance, to steal the next base and keep running. And some of them, against all logic, will make a homerun, just because they have the moxy to run the bases (and the other team is looking for the ball in a patch of weeds.)

What if every morning we adults woke up ready to make a homerun in our lives? What if our enthusiasm overruled our logic and propelled us to do great things for others and for God?

This prairie girl can imagine the Lord smiling when we give something our best, whether we are playing outfield, second base or it's our turn to bat. Like an engaged, doting parent or grandparent, I can almost hear Him shouting, "Go! Go!" We can be assured He is always on our team.

My devotional today stated, "The Bible calls you 'a child of God.' Stop and consider what that means. God's creativity is already built into your DNA; your job is to recognize it, release it, and put it to work." So what might happen to us, to our world, if we tap into our creative DNA?

The following verse became very real to me when I set out to publish *"By the Banks of Cottonwood Creek."* Recently I've been hearing or seeing it again almost every day. It feels like God's private word for me, but it is certainly a promise for everyone who trusts in Him.

> *"Being confident of this, that He who began a good work in you will carry it on to completion until the day of Christ Jesus."*
> *Philippians 1:6.*

That says to me I'm not alone in this life. If I trust Him, God will help me no matter what ball is thrown at me.

Wishing you all a joyride on a clover-scented day and a chance to hit a "homerun."

Where Every Bean is Gifted

Need a heart-warming story for a January day? Step inside the doors of The Gifted Bean Coffee House, a place overflowing with optimism, good will, and great coffee. Smiles are free and so are the clever sayings that show up in the shop and on their Facebook page.

Caution: Java installation 95% complete. Installation in progress.

The shop opened in Bismarck Public Library in October 2014, serving up coffee, lunch, the best chocolate chai ever (not just my opinion). On any given day, you may find friends chatting over fresh hot sandwiches, someone engrossed in a book, a writer at work, librarians rushing in to grab a cuppa, or maybe a party of individuals with unique abilities enjoying one of the games the shop has available.

However, to fully appreciate The Gifted Bean, you need to know that a "gifted bean" is really a "being who is gifted." This family-owned business has a larger purpose.

Matt and Sandy McMerty were a career-track couple when their first son was born 14 years ago with Down syndrome. They soon became involved in community efforts to support people with disabilities. However, they wanted Cristian to dream of a future of greater independence. They decided to find a business where he could work when he grew up to support that dream. When the shop became available, they saw it as it as "bean" their opportunity.

Their dream is becoming reality. Cristian, his parents and siblings all work in the shop, along with other staff, serving up great customer service. Recently, Cristian handed out his new business cards. They read, "Hello, I'm Cristian McMerty and I'm the future owner of The Gifted Bean, where every bean is special."

The McMerty's efforts are making a positive influence not just in Cristian's life, but throughout the community. Their inspiring story has been shared in TV, newspaper and magazine stories. In 2015, they were named Employer of the Year by The Arc of Bismarck for their contributions to the lives of people with disabilities.

When The Gifted Bean opened in 2014, I was still with The Library Foundation, working in the Library. Each morning I stopped by for a good cup of coffee and, well maybe, one of those fresh chocolate peanut butter bars.

Coffee and friends make the perfect blend.

Now that I'm retired from the Library, I'm still a weekly customer. After *By the Banks of Cottonwood Creek* was published last year, I stopped by for coffee and shared the news. To my surprise, they offered to sell the book, the first store in Bismarck to make it available. Now when I walk into the shop and a barista waves an envelope at me, I know they've sold another copy. It makes me happy, because it feels like they are on my team. And I am on theirs.

The Definition of Fear

This week I went to see the musical *Mary Poppins* at the Sleepy Hollow Theatre & Arts Park. On a perfect July evening, as the sun went down and the stars came out, a host of youth put on a stellar performance of the beloved musical.

I haven't seen *Mary Poppins* for a while and her practical wisdom surprised and delighted me. It made me think about learning to look past what I can see. Too often adversity and affliction block our view and blind us to the fact that good things can come out of trying situations. When we dwell on our problems, fear sets in and we are less likely to overcome them. We let our fears get the best of us!

Here is my favorite definition of FEAR: False Evidence Appearing Real.

Did you know a huge percentage of what we fear never happens? That is why it's so important to dwell on God's promises and tell ourselves the truth. Scriptures such as, "No weapon formed against you will prosper," Isaiah 54:17, and this one from Psalms 34:6, "This poor man cried, and the Lord heard him, and saved him out of all his troubles," can calm and encourage us.

Mary Poppins had lots of good advice. She said a spoonful of sugar could make the medicine go down in the most delightful way. Since we occasionally have to eat our words, we should make them sweet. In the New Living translation of the Bible, Proverbs 16:24 states that, "Kind words are like honey—sweet to the soul and healthy for the body." Our words are powerful! A few kind words can make someone's day and a good sense of humor can help us through almost any difficulty.

One of *Mary Poppins'* most memorable songs is, "Supercalifragilisticexpialidocious!" Richard M. Sherman, co-writer of the song, wryly observed that the definition of it, "was something to say when you have nothing to say."

Think about that. Instead of complaining when things don't go right, we should shout out, "supercalifragilisticexpialidocious!" We'd lift ourselves and everyone around us.

Grace Like Snow

All fall we had only a few drops of rain. The whole yard was dusty and dry, and dirt clung to the house and crept into every crevice. To make matters worse, a nearby retirement home has a building project going on with mountains of dirt that blow this way with every westerly gale.

I watered the trees and the perennials, washed windows, and hosed down the front porch, but it didn't seem to do much good. Out in the backyard, there was no getting rid of the grimy build up on the steps leading to the garden. Even the soft green moss that generally grows between the patio pavers turned gray. Freeze-dried perennials looked drab as they nodded in the wane autumn sun.

Then, the last week of November snow began to fall. Big, wet, white flakes feathered down from the sky. At first, the snow melted into the parched grass, but then it began to build up. An inch of snow. Eight inches of snow. Eighteen inches of snow. By early December, we had as much snow as we'd had all the winter before.

The mail truck couldn't get through, then school was cancelled, very rare occurrences in our normally dry climate. Adults groaned with the thought of digging out driveways and pushing their way through unplowed streets. Kids, on the other hand, could be seen outside in the worst of it, building snowmen or going sledding.

If you could see beyond the work and inconvenience, the city was prettier than any magazine photograph. The view from my office window, is of Colorado spruce and bull pine trees bowed under a blanket of sparkling white. Stepping outside you can smell evergreens, their refreshing fragrance released by the moisture.

I once had a revelation of what God's grace would look like if we could actually see it. I saw grace as white, pristine snow covering all of the less than beautiful parts of our lives. That was how He was seeing the world, seeing us, through the grace-filled covering His son Jesus provided for us.

Only heavenly beings and astronauts have seen the world from far away. James Irwin, a pilot on Apollo 15, said this about his flight into space, "The Earth reminded us of a Christmas tree ornament hanging in the blackness of space. As we got farther and farther away it diminished in size. Finally it shrank to the size of a marble, the most beautiful marble you can imagine."

David McCasland tells the story of astronaut Charles Frank Bolden's thoughts as he viewed the world from 400 miles up. It all looked peaceful and beautiful to him and he felt that he was viewing earth as it ought to be.

Earth as it ought to be. On earth as it is in heaven. Peaceful, beautiful, inspiring.

Maybe God is also looking down from heaven at this war torn world and His children carrying heavy burdens. Maybe he's saying, "Believe in Me, let your worries go, and ask for my help!"

I believe He has the power and the love to help us. I believe He's provided the grace to cover the burdens of yesterday, today and tomorrow. And just like the earth seems to sigh and rest under the weight of the snow, we can rest under His amazing grace.

Oh, to live like that, under the thick blanket of pure love and apply His grace to all of our shortcomings and worries. To quit shoveling through the messes in our lives and instead go hop in his sleigh and enjoy the wonders around us. So, let's release our burdens this Christmas and spend some time with Him. Let God's grace envelop you, and know that when he says, "Lo, I am with you always," that he means it. That is the message of Christmas delivered by the Messiah.

Personal Essays

Montana, the Coonhound & Me

Not many can say they spent their 12th birthday on a trip with four adults and a coonhound. Uncle Orville raised coonhounds and was delivering the pup, Homer, to a relative in Montana. He invited my family to ride along. The car was crowded with my uncle, aunt, Dad, Mom, me and Homer. Aunt Ianca didn't like dogs and I don't think my parents did either. Thus, before we began our 400-mile journey, Uncle Orville parked Homer's box on my lap.

"Oh goody," I said. Uncle Orville missed the sarcastic remark and Homer took the insult without a flinch.

This was before air-conditioning, but even with the windows rolled down, Homer gave off an ominous odor that all but gagged those of us in the backseat. In addition, for being half grown, he still had a lot of manners to learn.

It was my first honest to gosh trip to a ranch in Montana, Big Sky Country. Everything was out of proportion and a true wonder to me. Ranchers owned thousands of acres of land. The ranch where we stayed had 14 sections of land and hundreds of cattle. The house was done all in western décor; cowhide sofas and knotty pine furniture. The mammoth fireplace really impressed me. The new part of the house was attached to the original log cabin and that's where I slept.

Their neighbors were all characters that no imagination could make up. One was an elderly lady, complete with a Stetson hat and boots, that owned a whole township and was always involved in lawsuits. On the other side was a man who took a shotgun after the most innocent trespassers.

We visited one neighbor who lived along a creek among picturesque buttes. Their house was an authentic log cabin which had only recently been wired for electricity. They still used a cook stove and gas lights, an avocado green refrigerator being their only modern appliance.

Horseback riding in the peacefulness of the giant land and the happiness of knowing that as far as the eye could see, no man had walked, left a dent in my heart and an ache to return. Too soon we had to leave.

Getting into the car for the return trip home, my eyes met a somber face, a familiar one, that begged me to take him along. With a mixture of sadness and glee, I said, "Goodbye Homer."

That trip to Montana was long ago, but I still love the state and have taken many vacations there.

The Button Box

Like many women of my mother's generation, Mom kept a box filled with old buttons. On rainy days when I ran out of things to do, I could always go to the button box and sort the various shapes, sizes and colors.

Most of the buttons were white, but they were proof that there are many shades of white. Some had two holes, and some had four. Others had shanks underneath and required careful sewing.

In a time and place when ready-made clothes were hard to find and expensive, Mom sewed most of our dresses, shirts, and pajamas. She even sewed formal dresses, and one year she made a winter coat for me. She deftly made buttonholes for most garments and she could make covered buttons for high-end suits and dresses.

Recycling wasn't a hot topic back then. It was a way of life. Many of Mom's creations used recycled buttons and zippers. Buttons were snipped off and put in the button box for use on another piece of clothing. Zippers were ripped out and reused. She always had an assortment of rickrack, tape, snaps and hook fasteners.

Sewing was in her genes, as her mother and grandmother were excellent seamstresses. So were my sisters. Me, not so much.

Mom invested in a treadle sewing machine back in the 1930s when she had six young children. She probably made all of the girls' dresses, and perhaps, shirts for the boys. She continued to use that sewing machine until her death in 1986. In one of the drawers, we found the original purchase papers for the machine. She made the $5 monthly payment with money earned from selling eggs and cream.

Today when we tire of our clothes, we put them in a plastic bag or box and drop them off at a secondhand store. In my mother's day, when clothes wore out they went on to another life. Sometimes the piece was remodeled for another person. Wool and denim fabric became braided or woven rugs. Cotton was cut into squares and sewn into quilts that kept us warm in winter.

With so many stores closing and shipments unreliable, perhaps there will be a return to sewing your own clothes. If that happens, maybe the fancy sewing machine I bought to use during retirement will finally come out of the closet.

And maybe I had better start my own button box, just in case.

Canning Season

Here in North Dakota, we have five seasons: winter, spring, summer, fall, and canning season. Recently, when it was 98 degrees outside, a friend spent the day in the kitchen making beet pickles. Her joy in the finished product reminded me of my own canning roots.

However, I must confess, I've only made pickled beets once. Here's how you do it: First, you plant them in the garden and when they are grown you dig them out. Then they must be cleaned, boiled, peeled and sliced before the pickling process begins. When I got to that stage, I realized that beet juice makes wonderful dye for hands, clothes and the kitchen.

We had no air conditioning in those days and the windows were open. I could hear the kids having fun as they ran through the sprinkler. I considered dumping the whole beet project and joining them, especially after I found out an ingredient was missing. However, duty called, so I loaded the wet kids in the car for a trip to the store, where I walked past the jars of beet pickles to get to the spice aisle.

Another canning story happened on a steamy August day when I was a kid. Mom was canning green beans in our farm kitchen. I was sent outside to hang around with Dad. That's when the accident happened.

To summarize, let's just say I was seven year old with very good intentions when I put the pickup in reverse and drove over the junk pile.

When the pickup finally stopped, all four tires were flat, and there was a cream can wedged under the front bumper. (You just can't make up details like that, can you?) Anyway, Dad sent me to the kitchen to confess to Mom, who turned off the gas stove, released the pressure valve on the canner, and came outside to help pry the pickup out. For the rest of the afternoon, I sat on the shop step and listened to Mom bawl me out as they sweated over the mess I made.

Although, I haven't driven a pickup in years and no longer do much canning, when I do I think of Mom and the beans. Today, my summer tradition is limited to occasional batches of corn relish, apple butter, salsa, or cherries. In a good apple year, there will also be apple pies in the freezer.

We are blessed to have an abundant supply of fresh fruits and vegetables from all over the world, something I couldn't have imagined as a child. I hadn't actually seen empty grocery shelves in decades, until the coronavirus appeared. It made me appreciate what many people in the world deal with on a regular basis.

For most of history, food was locally grown. People raised their own meat, grain, veggies and fruits. Late summer and fall were dedicated to bringing in the harvest and preserving it. Many homes had a storehouse or cellar that could hold a winter's worth of potatoes, carrots, squash, and shelves of canned good.

Preserving foods was the thrifty and healthy way to go. The movement to support locally grown foods is a good one, and perhaps it's also time to consider preserving and storing food again. However, I'm not likely to be pickling beets any time soon.

Almost everyone knows the Lord's Prayer, but how often do we think about its meaning? One line states, *"Give us this day our daily bread."* Matt. 6:11, NKJV. Only when the shelves were empty, did I really think about that and changed that daily prayer. Now I say, "thank you for the incredible amount of food you have blessed us with."

Picnic Table Lessons

It had come to this: either scrape and repaint the picnic table or haul it to the curb for trash pickup. The redwood table and benches had been part of the family for decades, an unassuming presence at birthday parties, Fourth of July celebrations and at least one Easter dinner. But now, the paint peeled in some places, while the wood rotted in others.

It was a come-to-Jesus moment for the table. Was it still worth the cost of a bucket of paint or was it past redemption? Perhaps it deserved another chance, I decided, perhaps it still had a few good years left in it. I bought some paint and invited our grandsons over for an afternoon project.

It took the three of us several hours to restore the table. And while it may always have the aura of an old table, but it is useful once again.

In the restoration process, I realized the table is a lot like we humans. We are also aged by time and the stresses of life, but just as we can restore an old picnic table or other items, God is about the business of saving us from the proverbial trash heap. Here are some lessons gleaned from the table:

1. From a distance, the table appeared to be "shabby chic," but up close you could see it was old, dirty and in need of repair. Sometimes we think our attitudes and actions are trendy, when they are instead corrupt and keep us from a life rich in blessing. *"Do not conform any longer to the pattern to this world, but be transformed by the renewing of your mind." Romans 12:2* *

2. The table couldn't clean itself up. Like we humans, it didn't have the power to restore itself. Neither do we have the power to overcome the failures in our lives without help. Like King David, we need to say, *"Create in me a clean heart, O God, and renew a right spirit within me." Psalm 51:10 ESV.*

3. Cold water from the hose. A wire brush. Sandpaper. A scraper. If the table had been alive, it might have cried, "Ouch! Quit it! I'd rather be in the landfill than go through this." It can also be painful to accept change in our lives, because too often we see change as the end, rather than the beginning. *"My son, do not despise the Lord's discipline and do not resent his rebuke, because the Lord disciplines those he loves, as a father the son he delights in." Proverbs 3:11-12*

4. It was plain to see how dirt was destroying the picnic table, so we carefully covered every part with paint: the legs, between the boards, the corners underneath. Sometimes the little hidden things in our lives are destructive, like the dirt between the cracks in the picnic table. The Bible calls them the "little foxes" or secret sins. *"Catch for us the foxes, the little foxes that ruin the vineyards." Song of Solomon 2:15.*

5. A coat of paint covered the table's flaws, just as the redeeming power of Jesus' death on the cross covers over our sins and makes up for our shortcomings. *"If we confess our sins he is faithful and just and will forgive us our sins and purify us from all unrighteousness." I John 1:9*

Over the years, the picnic table has received numerous coats of paint, so this was just one of many times that it has been restored. Thank God, he never gives up on us, either, whether it's the second, third, for forty-third time we need his cleansing and forgiving coat of grace.

"Therefore, if anyone is in Christ, the new creation has come: The old has gone, the new is here!" II Cor. 5: 17.

The Ice Cream Bar

Today, I bought a box of ice cream bars, and the first bite transported me back to the dusty main street of Dickey, North Dakota.

When I was growing up, my parents and I often drove to Dickey on Sunday afternoons to see Dad's family. From our farm, it was a straight shot north on a gravel road. As we drove, the flat land dipped into the fertile James River Valley. Today, the valley is part of the Chan SanSan Scenic Backway. Back then, we just thought it was pretty.

Along the way, we'd pass the farm where Dad's parents had lived, though they were gone before I was born. The Larsons had arrived at Dickey in 1902, and decades later many of Dad's siblings still lived in the area. Sisters Mary, Ella, Emma and Lillie all lived in Dickey at that time.

I remember asking Dad how they traveled when they moved from southern Minnesota. With a straight face, he said with a team of oxen. That gave me a lot of food for thought. I was grown up before I realized he was joking and that settlers of that era arrived by train.

Dickey is a village of gravel streets and unpretentious houses. Ella lived in a low rambling brown stucco house on the main street, along with Aunt Emma. The adults would gather around the round oak dining room table with cups of coffee and oatmeal cookies or rhubarb cake.

One hot late summer day when we went to Dickey, one of my aunts took pity on me being the only child present and gave me a nickel to buy ice cream. I was so sheltered. At seven-year-old I'd never been sent off alone in a strange town. Although the town had fewer than a hundred people, it seemed big to me. I bravely walked a block or so up the street, the blue sky above framed by golden-hewed elm and cottonwood trees, the hot wind throwing sand at my bare legs.

I've always thought I went to a little general store, but the state's blue laws were in effect, so it must have been a café. You know the kind, it had a big front window, a squeaky screen door, a floor fan blowing inside. A long freezer with a slide door on the top stood against one wall.

They didn't have ice cream cones, so I picked out a Cherrio, which I had always wanted to try. Plopping my nickel on the counter and headed back to Aunt Ella's. Within a minute in the hot sun, ice cream was leaking out of the paper wrapper. I opened it up and began damage control, slurping at the chocolate and vanilla treat, trying not to get any on my clothes.

Until writing this story, I didn't realize the subconscious choices I make when writing, for the towns in my books are a lot like Dickey and Adrian, an even smaller village that is a seven mile drive west through the pristine valley.

In *By the Banks of Cottonwood Creek, Amber's Choice,* and *Cottonwood Dreams,* the village of Schulteville was named after my Aunt Lillie and Uncle Adrian Schulte. At the time of the Cheerio meltdown, they lived in a rambling one-story hot pink house a few blocks from Ella's. Later they moved to Adrian (yes, Adrian moved to Adrian).

Still later they bought the nicest house in Dickey, a square two-story dune-colored stucco house. The attic was as large as any house we had lived in and a covered porch ran across the front of the house.

It still stands across the street from the Methodist church.

In the books, I put Aunt Kate in the nicest house in Schulteville and located it across the street from the church. However the fictional Aunt Kate Schulte has a tart tongue while my Aunt Lillie was the sweetest.

The Friendship Ring

Back in the day before mood rings, promise rings, and nose rings, there were friendship rings. These silver bands were popular with the junior high crowd, and girls gave them to each other for birthday or Christmas gifts.

While most of my friends proudly wore friendship rings, no one gave one to me and I felt bad about it. Then on my 14th birthday, I received a silver friendship ring with a heart at its center and one on each side! It was one of the nicer friendship rings I'd seen.

What I didn't want to admit was who had given it to me: my mother. How embarrassing!

Classmate: Nice friendship ring! Look at those neat hearts! Who gave it to you?

Me: Mumble, mumble.

Classmate: Who?

Me: My mother.

Classmate: Oh. Gotta go now.

The irony was that Mom and I didn't have a warm mother-daughter relationship. How I wished for "heart to heart" talks with Mom, as Sandra Dee and Annette Funicello had with their mothers in the movies, but Mom was closed to such nonsense. Instead, as I grew up she became the patrol officer, while I donned a black jacket and boots and took to smoking Winstons.

After I married and had a family, we got along better. We visited her on weekends and spend holidays together. When it became harder for our family to get away, Mom seemed to understand. She worked until she was 73, traveled, made quilts, and did the one thing she said she'd never do—have coffee klatches with friends.

Mom died in 1986. Since then, much too late, I have gained more understanding of my mother. The hardships she and Dad faced as they raised my siblings during the Depression. The dreams that blew away during the Dirty Thirties. Raising a late baby (me) while my father's health failed. Perhaps most difficult, the hope she must have lost for the future.

Mom never said, "You did a good job," "I love you" or "follow your dreams." Forget smiles or hugs. Instead, Mom did her best for me by making complete wardrobes for my dolls. She provided money for milk at school and for "bank day" savings, even when her pay check hardly covered the rent. She also paid for art lessons while I was in high school. And she gave me a friendship ring.

Today, the ring is a reminder that not everyone communicates in the same way. Sometimes we must listen with our hearts rather than our ears.

I still have the friendship ring. Its sterling silver hearts have a patina now, and surprisingly, it still fits my finger. Through it, Mom seems to reach out to me across time. I'm honored to tell people it was a gift from a good friend: my mother.

But don't just listen to God's word. You must do what it says. Otherwise, you are only fooling yourselves. James 1:22 NLT

The River's Edge

I t's a bright, chilly June day. I'm lagging behind on a walk through the sand dunes on the west side of the Missouri River.

My husband and I had offered our grandsons, ages 14 and 19, a day trip. They turned down Medora, Fargo and other destinations for a trip to the beach.

Nothing could please me more. We've made an annual pilgrimages to this serene and little known place below Garrison Dam for decades. It's my favorite spot on earth. If they can't find a place to bury me someday, they should just stick my body here in a sand dune.

I trudge up a hill of sugar-fine sand, skid down the other side, and then push up the next one. Suddenly, I'm overlooking the Missouri. The river laps by as green as a wall of ivy. The cerulean blue sky reaches down to the craggy bluffs on the other side.

Later I'll catch up with the others. For now, I'm alone in the quiet. The uncommon quiet. No wisp of wind, no cry of shore bird, no human voice. Just perfect stillness. I collapse to the ground and brace my hands in the warm sand. The silence empties my soul of the high frequency noise that fills my life. Below, the water is so clear that you can see coal-laced grains of sand all the way to where the shelf drops into the river's deep channel.

This beach has been featured in three of my books, and as I immerse myself in the view, my characters are with me. We are like quiet old friends sharing a sacred place. Throughout the Prairie Pastor series, Kelly Jorgenson often found solace here.

In the second book, Amber's Choice, one chapter is even entitled Down by the River. In that chapter, he found a forty-foot log, sat down on it and dug his feet into the cool, damp sand.

I remove my shoes and bury my toes in the sand. How many times have I sat pondering on that same log where Kelly sat? It remained anchored on the river's edge for several years. This year, however, the river has shifted. The log may still lay on the other side of a cliffy bluff, but the bank seems too unstable to check it out. A number of ancient trees have lost their grip and lay with their massive roots thrust over the river.

Later, I'll wander back to my guys. They have staked out a place next to the water's edge. There, the boys dig waist-deep holes and flood a series of dikes, while their grandpa sleeps in the sun and I read a book.

The river shifts like a person in an uncomfortable bed. For a few years, there were warm pools of clean warm water where we could swim. Other years were great for catching little frogs. Then in 2011, the river flooded. Water poured in from the Montana mountains in record-breaking amounts. The lake behind Garrison Dam rose. And rose.

For the first time in its sixty years, water flowed over the spillway of the dam. We went to look at it on July Fourth that year, marveling at the thunder of the water trying to break free of the dam. There was no beach to visit.

Since then, the bank has continued to erode and the wetlands between the parking lot and river are dry and full of reeds. Still, we've been able to find some beach space. And for a few hours we abandon ourselves to the sun and sand and silent powerful beauty of the Missouri.

Anniversary Grace

The electric frying pan and coffeepot have gone to appliance heaven, but 50 years after our wedding, we still use a CorningWare casserole, metal mixing bowls and aluminum cookware that were opened on our wedding day. We still have a blue-flowered blanket, a Fostoria serving bowl (used twice) and a picture of Jesus. And we still have each other.

Our wedding was in January, right after a real North Dakota blizzard. When I woke that morning in my parents' home, the sun was shining and the window glowed with Jack Frost's artwork. The bright sky seemed like a good sign.

My dad was sitting at the kitchen table. He said, "Well, I guess I'll go to the wedding." It still makes me cry to think how he must have wanted to walk his youngest daughter down the aisle. Dad had a stroke when I was 16. On my wedding day, he was just out of the hospital again and quite frail. I had expected my oldest brother to do the honors.

Meanwhile, the groom was braving the not-plowed-out roads to Oakes, 25 miles away, to pick up the flowers for the wedding. He made it to the church early, with fresh, not frozen, flowers. That was feat in his red '65 Mustang. The sun was out, but the thermometer hovered near 30 below.

The little brown brick church was a warm place to say our vows. Then we strolled next door to the reception in the church hall. Larry's family supplied the ham and homemade wedding kuchen. My family supplied the buns and wedding cake, baked at Elmer's Bakery where my mother worked. In a corner of the hall, our sisters unwrapped the wedding gifts.

At the time, I really couldn't see past the first few days of marriage and only knew how nice it would be to wake up together each morning. I certainly didn't consider spending 50 years together. I didn't even know anyone who had reached their golden anniversary.

The wedding vows made when you're young and naïve take on new meaning when your marriage spans decades. For better, for worse. We've had whole seasons that were awesome and whole seasons that were…worse. For richer, for poorer. In sickness and in health. We've done it all, except for death do us part. We hope to wait a while on that one.

But we haven't done it alone. We have a Friend who has been part of our marriage from the beginning. Even on our honeymoon we attended church, and some of our best moments have been when we've prayed together.

In addition, friends and family have helped us over the rough spots, given us encouragement and led by example. To all of them we say thank you. To my bridesmaid, I say thank you for a lifetime of friendship. Larry's best man has passed away, but the last time we visited him he begged us to appreciate each other and cherish each day. His wife was gone, his days were numbered, and his wisdom flowed like a fountain.

We did the big dinner at the country club for our 40th and once was enough. For our 50th we are celebrating more quietly. Friends have already taken us to dinner, and on the anniversary date we will dine at a nice restaurant with our sons, daughter-in-law and grandsons. We'll look through our wedding book and watch the DVD of our 40th anniversary celebration. It is enough.

Here is a special verse from Isaiah 43: 19: *See, I am doing a new thing! Now it springs up; do you not perceive it? I am making a way in the wilderness and streams in the wasteland.*

If God has the power to help two green kids through 50 years of marriage, he also has the power to help all of us find grace, peace and joy promised those who ask Him into their hearts.

The Muir Guest House

One hundred years ago today if you'd knocked on the door of what is now the Muir Guest House in LaMoure, N.D., Bessie Muir would have opened the door and welcomed you into the front porch.

She might have been holding baby June, while little Donald, 4, played nearby. Neva, 7, and Margaret, 6, would have been in school, while her husband, Gale, was off doing carpentry. You might have spied her sewing machine near a window, with a piece of fabric still under the needle. In the kitchen, perhaps bread baked in the old-fashioned oven.

Last year, Bessie and Gale's granddaughter and her husband, Nick and Judy Muir Meisch, purchased the property. Since then, Judy has invested much thought and energy in providing an attractive, comfortable place to stay for people visiting LaMoure.

Judy and I share an intrigue with the Muir family history. About 10 years ago Bessie and Gale's son, Wallace Muir (1921-2008), published *The Muir-Kloubec Genealogy and History 1708-2005*. I was lucky enough to help him with the editing after he spent 20 years doing the research and writing.

My heart was captured by the story of Bessie's early years. She grew up with one family crisis after another, and yet became a woman of kindness, humor and hardiness. How did she overcome the painful secrets she locked away in her heart? Based on Uncle Wallace's research, I spent seven years writing Bessie's coming of age story. It will be published one of these days. *(Note: Secrets of the Dark Closet, Second Edition is available online.)*

A few years ago Judy also purchased another house owned by Bessie and Gale. One they lived in for decades, located two doors west of the Muir Guest House. This is the house where we cousins remember enjoying many happy family gatherings. Bessie and Gale moved there in 1919 because they were outgrowing their "tiny" house. Ironically, this house isn't much bigger than the other, but they managed to raise eight kids there.

I'm proud of our family history, not because any-one was rich, famous or powerful (although there is that longshot connection to the Muir Castle in Scotland), but because they were people of hope, faith and integrity.

Congratulations Judy and Nick on the opening of the Muir Guest House. See what it looks like at www.Facebook.com/Muirguesthouse.

Here is one of my all-time favorite quotes: *"Every life is the result of series of choices and crossroads— not only ours, but those of our ancestors for genera- tions behind us. In the present, as in the past, each individual holds a key to the future. We stand at the crossroads of our personal histories and the deci- sions we make set into motion values and attitudes that affect not only our own development as men and women made in the image of God, but the choices and decisions that will face our descendants for genera- tions to come."* Michael Phillips and Judith Pella in *The Stonewyke Legacy.*

Big Sky Country

The phrase Big Sky Country was coined by A.B. Guthrie in his book by the same name. Later it was made into a movie.

Driving back across North Dakota in the evening, this prairie state is also big sky country. We watch the billowing clouds east of us a hundred, maybe two hundred miles away. As the Interstate turns this way and that, but always in on an easterly course, we wonder at the location of the clouds. North of Bismarck or south?

Above us, the great big blue bowl of a sky, the same color as a robin's egg, stretches out so vast that a train with a hundred cars looks like a Z-scale toy. Grain elevators, trucks, and farm equipment look like the toys farms so popular when I was a kid.

I wish I could describe the lush green pastures and golden grain fields, but alas, they country is instead baked to dust under the merciless sun. It is 103 degrees with gusts of wind that bump at the car like a belligerent bully. We drive past abandoned farm buildings, a reminder of the death of dreams past.

And yet the future rolls into view. Rows of gleaming wind generators turn in the persistent wind, while communication towers balance atop brown buttes.

This part of the heartland is treeless, except for those trees planted and nurtured by the people who believed, who still believe in a future here. Magnificent herds of cattle lean to the ground pulling at the prairie grasses. We drove across the country from the

East Coast a few years ago and it isn't until we got to North Dakota that you see large herds of cattle.

The Bible says that God owns the cattle on a thousand hills. Those words must have been prophetic, for surely those ancient writers had not seen such a sight, but by faith understood the vastness of the world, the vastness of this land where thousands and thousands of cattle range on as many hillsides. In the vastness of time, families rise and then dissipate like the fluff of thistle, but the land remains through wet and dry years.

To the southwest, a pale three-quarter moon floats in the sky. It's dimmed by the sun, which still reigns in the west, although it is almost 9 p.m. Last evening, after a full day at Yellowstone Park, we were back at the hotel before the Independence Day fireworks began. The sun had set in the west, leaving layers of color behind. A tangerine sky topped the jagged violet mountains. Against this background, fireworks exploded in red, white and blue. It is a scene that could only happen in a place with a big sky.

Big sky country is the epitome of the big idea, of America, a place of freedom and vast opportunity. That idea grabbed the hearts of our Founding Fathers. Through the centuries, countless immigrants seized the idea of big hope. Indeed, in America's first national park (Yellowstone, 1872) on this Fourth of July, the crowds of people more often than not spoke in a foreign language. Whether they were visitors or new Americans we did not know. What is known is that they chose to travel to the heart of North America. Perhaps like me, they were intrigued with the vast beauty and potential of America.

Holidays

Sad Ritual, New Year

On January 1, 2019, I opened the family Bible and recorded my brother's death. Robert Allen Larson died on Christmas Eve at the age of 86. He led a full life and will be remembered for his stories, humor, wisdom and work ethic. He and Margaret were married for 66 years and they had seven children, eight grandchildren, and a number of great grandchildren.

That he made it to a good old age is remarkable with his track record. He fell out of a second story window when he was a toddler, but was unhurt. When he was five, a barn door fell on his leg. That time, he spent three weeks in a cast in a hospital bed in a sweltering upstairs room. He also fell through the ice on Cottonwood Creek as a boy, and was fished out by his younger brother.

That same Cottonwood Creek appears in my historical novel *Secrets of the Dark Closet*. That's because my siblings grew up on the old Muir farm where my great grandfather settled and where my mother was born.

By the time I came along, the family had moved to a farm a few miles away. The house was too small for a large family. After that, Bob mostly lived with other families and worked for board and room while he finished school.

That work ethic was lifelong. After he was drafted into the Army, he learned to drive heavy equipment in France. He went on to own a construction company, and had a hobby farm. In late 2018 when he was 85, his son recorded a video of Bob loading giant hay bales onto a truck bed with his favorite tractor.

Last May we stopped to visit Bob and Margaret at their farm home near Edgeley. Bob was eager to show us around. We didn't know, as we rode around in his Polaris utility vehicle, that it was the last quality time we would spend together.

As we drove around, we saw his life described in the equipment, buildings and belongings set around the farmstead.

After Dad died in 1971, Bob served as the unofficial head of the family. His quiet wisdom was a guiding force. I shall probably always ask myself the question, "What would Bob do?" when a problem arises.

That New Year's Day, I added to the family record in a small black leather Bible. But first I turned to the front where these words are inscribed: "Birthday Greetings Sept. 19, 1937 from Mother." The Bible was a personal gift from my grandmother to Dad. It is the only example of her handwriting, neat and upright, that I've ever seen. Andreana Larson died before I was born.

The Family Register rests between Malachi and Matthew. The handwriting in it is revealing. Dad's awkward scrawl, not unlike mine, recorded his name, birth date, and the names of his parents.

Then, my mother's clean Palmer Method penmanship took over. On the Births page, the names of my three sisters and three brothers were all recorded with the same pen and type of ink. They were born so close together. My birth was recorded in a later decade with a different pen. The Marriages page is the most fun to read. Each of the new brides in our family recorded the couples full names and wedding date.

Adding Bob's name to the Deaths page felt like a sacred moment. He is now listed with my parents, and all of my sisters and brothers. I'm not comfortable being the last one living, but am resigned to my role as keeper of the family history. It won't be a lonely job, because my nieces and nephews share in the role.

Today we are overwhelmed with advertisements, messages, emails and other forms of communication. Yet, there is little regard for written records these days.

How many families keep a family Bible? Wedding books and baby books have gone out of style. Letter writing is a vanishing art. Good punctuation is unnecessary in social media. Obituaries often include the name of the deceased person's dog, but forget to put in the dates of their birth and death.

The same goes for photographs. I have a drawer full of old photos. Most of them are a single recording of an event. Today, instead of taking one good photo, people take thousands, and then neglect to even store them in "the cloud."

Our family Bible, gifted over eighty years ago, seems like a small thing as it sits on the bookshelf. Yet, it contains so much. Along with a brief record of our family's history, it is a message from my grandmother: that she respected the Word of God and wanted to pass it on.

Easter Grace

Happy Easter! Do you have a favorite Easter memory? One of mine is of sharing Easter breakfast with the members of the Youth Fellowship group when I was a teen. We met at the parsonage. Think about that a minute. It's Easter, a busy day for pastors, and our pastor and his wife had five kids. Still, they graciously invited a bunch of teens over for Easter breakfast. I might add that some of us were dressed in our finest patent leather 1-inch pumps and some of the boys were pretty rowdy (you know who you are.)

One year, I volunteered to bring Easter Lilies, a delicacy created by my mother by baking individual sponge cakes one at a time on oven-proof saucers. This treat was just made at Easter and she usually sent small boxes of them to my sisters who couldn't come home for the holiday.

When I told Mom I had volunteered her to make 15 for the breakfast, she had to sit down for a minute and recover from the shock. Then she dutifully baked enough for the whole group. (She didn't trust me to do the baking, but I got to help frost them and put the orange slice in.) I'm so pleased that a number of my nieces carry on the tradition of making Easter Lilies.

This Prairie Girl is really into Easter traditions. I love Palm Sunday. On that day long ago, people were praising Jesus. The Bible says if they wouldn't have praised Him, the very rocks would have cried out. This year on Palm Sunday our children's pastor and a bevy of kids belted out a song that had the whole congregation standing to its feet cheering, like on the original Palm Sunday.

Each year, I read through a gospel account of the passion and resurrection of Christ. Reading about the betrayal, mock trial and death of Jesus is hard, but the bitterness of that story makes the resurrection so much more wonderful. It shows us that there is hope even in our darkest hours, when we think all is lost.

The tradition I like best is attending church on Easter morning. The earlier the better. There is often an eagerness to the service, as though Jesus has just risen from the grave and we, his disciples, are coming to celebrate. I always hope we sing Christ the Lord Is Risen Today, which Charles Wesley first published in 1739. The music and words are so powerful that almost three hundred years later, I can't sing it without being choked up.

The message of Easter is multifaceted, but it can be boiled down to this one word: Hope. Jesus Christ brings new hope for each of us. On Easter, we pause to honor our Lord because we are forgiven, set free, and renewed by grace.

So, dear readers, may you find fresh joy in the Easter message this year and don't forget to sprinkle the holiday with some tradition. Dye eggs on Good Friday. Have some raisin sauce with your Easter ham. Or enjoy a sunrise service.

Hebrews 10: 23 states, "Let us hold unswervingly to the hope we profess for he who promised is faithful."

This Mom was Always Out of Step

This month we celebrate Mother's Day, and so Happy Mother's Day to all your mothers, grandmothers, aunts and women who fill in when a mom isn't present. You have the most important role in the world.

That said, I'd like to ponder why I was mostly out of step with other mothers of my generation. It's true and here is why. Back when other women were out burning bras and demanding rights, I was a stay-at-home mom with bands of preschoolers stopping by the kitchen for fresh baked cookies. Plus, I was obsessed with providing balanced meals for my family every night. (Eat your peas!) Later, I was a CCD teacher and carpool driver.

I wasn't the perfect mother. The kids would probably say I was closer to Mommy Dearest than Ma Ingalls, but I was there and I hope that counts a little. My world looked much different than Gloria Steinem's, but I wouldn't have traded those years for a corner office anywhere.

Still, I secretly longed for a career someday. But, how could I manage when there were skinned knees to bandage? Lots of them. And Tough Skin jeans to return to Sears. Now that I think about it, I bet there was a correlation there between those knees and my most frequent words. "Ouch! Didn't I tell you to pick up the Legos?"

Later, instead of engaging in discussions about women's roles, I was influenced by the gray-haired ladies in my life. They helped me through a long stretch of time, including the three-year period when my mother and sisters died. These women weren't trying to break the glass ceiling. They were going beyond the ceiling to touch the throne of God with their prayers, and they invited me along.

Their love and kindness nurtured this lost prairie girl. Lucille and Flora, Cary Lou and Sister Susan. They offered encouragement, advice, stories from their own lives. And Elenor, a Bible study leader who was in her 70s. Every day she walked two miles and did pushups. And every day she prayed for all the girls who had attended her classes through the years. Imagine remembering our names for so long.

What great role models they and others were. Those gray-haired ladies lived out a counter culture right in the heart of Bismarck. Successful in their own right, they made my life richer because they lived fully in the life God gave them. They strengthened, encouraged and taught us what a woman should be and do.

They taught by word and example that God has a higher call on our lives. That we are special. That we matter in a world caught up in media blitz and Hollywood gossip.

There are many other women who were mentored by those gray-haired ladies. With the hindsight of many years I can look back and say that they chose a life of service and, because of that, their quiet influence is still having an impact. I can see the results in the families of the "girls" they mentored, who found a new way of living.

Today not so many women let their hair go gray, but we can still have an impact on younger women who need a mom or just need to see a steady strength which comes from being deeply planted in the things of God. So, to every woman who has come along side to help me or to help other women, Happy Mother's Day!

If you long for the kind of influence these gray-haired ladies gave, consider attending a women's Bible study at a local church or join a women's fellowship group, such as Christian Women's Clubs. Women's retreats or conferences are a great place to nurture your soul. Take a friend or go by yourself and look for someone you can befriend.

> *"Your beauty should not come from outward adornment, such as elaborate hairstyles and the wearing of gold jewelry or fine clothes. 4 Rather, it should be that of your inner self, the unfading beauty of a gentle and quiet spirit, which is of great worth in God's sight."*
> *I Peter 3: 3-4*

"Each time we cooperate with God, we take one more giant step forward. Because when God asks us to change, it means that He always has something better to give us - more freedom, greater joy, and greater blessings." Joyce Meyer

It Almost Always Rains on Memorial Day

It almost always rains on Memorial Day,
As the skies open up, a gray-haired man stands
Tall in the uniform he can still button
And blows a bugle sounding taps.

In front of the American Legion building,
As the flag raises with creaking chains pulling it up.
Or in a national cemetery, where sound rolls across acres
Of white crosses shining against spring grass.

Or a country cemetery guarded by a wrought iron fence
And decorated with bright plastic flowers,
Purchased at the local hardware store.
The place matters not, as hearts remember, remember.

It almost always rains on Memorial Day,
As the 21-gun salute to the fallen pierces the air
Shot off by men who wrest guns to their tired shoulders
And boys who hardly need to shave.

As rain drops fall and thunder booms overhead,
A deafening symphony saluting all who gave their lives
To save the one thing so important that a man will lay down
The joy of a quiet life and home and family and job.

It almost always rains on Memorial Day,
Great drops from leaden skies as heaven cries for those
Who fought and died for freedom and those whose hobbling gate
Ensured the freedom to pursue life and liberty.

And mothers and fathers and brothers and sisters and
Wives and children who touch faded photos,
And open a box of medals to remember
How their lives were never, never the same again.

But, perhaps it doesn't always rain on Memorial Day,
Perhaps what falls from heaven are the tears of those
Who have gone before us or the angels themselves
Whose water is shed on crowds gathered in sacred honor.

Or weeping families driven brutally from their homes,
Who perish before their time in each other's arms,
Yearning, yearning for peace on earth as it is in heaven
To live in freedom with each other and with our Maker.

A Father's Day Chat for Dads

It's the middle of June, a time to celebrate Father's Day, so here is a simple thought for you: Dads, you are really important to your children!

That might seem obvious, but in this crazy mixed up world, fathers can't be blamed for wondering if they count. To some, the traditional family seems old-fashioned as people opt to marry later in life, not marry at all, or marry someone of the same sex.

Raising kids is hard. Sometimes they don't listen to you. They make messes. *In addition, sometimes the little dears act just like you.* No, being a father isn't for the faint-hearted. It takes courage to stay with the job.

Right here I need to say thank you to my own father. He saved me from a gander when I was six, came to my room and listened sympathetically to my side of a dispute with Mom when I was a teenager, and walked me down the aisle on my wedding day when he probably should have been in the hospital. I miss you Dad, and I wish we could have had more time together.

We humans have a built-in longing for our father's approval and guidance. It's as strong as our need for food, water and air. Some people spend their whole lives searching for a meaningful relationship with a father figure, it's that important.

The average dad doesn't have a diploma or certification to do the job. Men come with a range of fathering abilities. Some walk away from their children, leaving their offspring to forever wonder why. Others provide for their children's every physical and emotional need. Most fathers fall somewhere in the middle, doing the best they can with what they've been given.

But, maybe children's needs are bigger than what a mere father can provide. French philosopher Blaise Pascal said this: *"There is a God shaped vacuum in the heart of every man which cannot be filled by any created thing, but only by God, the Creator, made known through Jesus."*

Maybe we ask too much of our fathers, when what we really need is to go to our heavenly Father. God knew us before we were born. He wants a relationship with us. He is willing and able to help us. We can tell Him what is on our hearts and He will whisper His love in our ear.

So all you dads out there, take heart. You have an important job, but you don't have to play God. Instead, you can turn to Him as a ready source of wisdom for your role as father.

For down-to-earth help with parenting, check out these books: *"The Five Love Languages of Children"* by Gary Chapman; *"Bringing Up Boys"* by James C. Dobson; or *"Have a New Kid By Friday"* by Kevin Leman. Each of these men have a proven record in helping families.

"As a father has compassion on his children,
so the Lord has compassion on those who
fear him." Psalm 103:13.

Born on the 4th of July

Yep! Uncle Sam and I were both born on July 4. That should give me an inside track on American history, yes? But, no, last February when preparing for a President's Day talk, I learned how much I've forgotten about Independence Day!

Sometimes I wonder what today's students know about the past, but now I wonder, could I pass a test on Early American History?

Twentieth Century writer and philosopher George Santayana said, "Those who cannot remember the past are condemned to repeat it." The bottom line is the Pilgrims came to America in 1620 both for freedom and to practice their faith freely. This is something we need to keep fresh and alive in our minds, lest we forget why and how this nation began.

In 1776, when leaders from the 13 colonies declared independence from Britain, the desire for freedom still ruled. That's when the details of the U.S. Constitution were hammered out. The Bill of Rights was added a few years later. It's first article states that "Congress shall make no law respecting the establishment of religion, or prohibiting the free exercise thereof, or bridging the freedom of speech, or of the press; or the right of the people to peaceably to assemble, and to petition the government for a redress of grievances."

Here is a short test on America's birth for you to try out:

What was the first item of business when the first Continental Congress met on Sept. 6, 1774? Answer:

They opened with prayer and read chapters from the Bible, including Psalm 35.

Who drafted the constitution? Answer: Thomas Jefferson drafted the U.S. Constitution in June of 1776.

Why did 40 leaders from the 13 colonies meet in Philadelphia on July 2, 1776? Answer: To approve a complete separation from Great Britain and the tyranny of government.

After days of deliberation in a hot, stuffy room, when did they approve U.S. Constitution? Answer: On July 4, 1776.

What did they do to mark the occasion? Answer: On July 8th, they carried the Declaration of Independence outside Independence Hall. There they read it to the assembled crowd and rang the Liberty Bell.

What is the inscription on the Liberty Bell? Answer:

"Proclaim liberty throughout the land, to all the inhabitants thereof." (Leviticus 25: 10.)

How many times during the American Revolution, did the Continental Congress issued proclamations for prayer? Answer: 15 times they made prayer proclamations appealing for God's help or in thanksgiving.

How many of the 56 signers of the Declaration of Independence were graduates of what would now be considered Bible schools or seminaries? Answer: Over half.

What is inscribed on every major building in Washington, D.C.? Answer: Scripture.

How did you do? Give yourself one point for each correct answer.

Remembering Veterans
of the Korean War

The Korean War Memorial in Washington, D.C., brings home the reality of war like none other. Dedicated in 1995, it includes 19 stainless steel statues, a mural wall, a United Nations wall and a reflecting pool.

The statues depict troops moving through a rice paddy in Korea. The statues are riveting during the day and downright eerie at night. The larger than life figures from the Army, Marines, Navy and Air Force are dressed in full combat gear. No matter where you stand, one of these statues is looking right at you.

The wall is 164 feet long and has 2,500 photographic images sandblasted into it of land, sea and air troops. You can touch the photographed faces of men who fought in Korea.

We don't talk about the Korean War very much, even though over 54,000 Americans died there. I found it sobering to read the names of soldiers who died, were wounded or went missing in action. They are listed on granite blocks near the pool at the memorial.

Korea was divided during World War II. It officially became two countries in 1948. Then in 1950, China and Russia invaded South Korea. Eventually 21 countries came to South Korea's defense. The United States provided 88 percent of the support troops. The war ended in 1953.

Since then, an intense contrast can be seen in the progress of each country. South Korea is a democracy with the thirteenth strongest economy in the world. Its 50 million people value education. About 30 percent of the people are Christian. The rapid rise in the standard of living and economic expansion have been dubbed the Miracle on the Han River. Think Samsung, LG and Hyundai. Per capita income in South Korea is over $28,000 per year.

North Korea has been ruled by despots since the end of the war. It has the worst human rights record in the world. Whisper something against the government and you are likely to find yourself in a harsh work camp without the benefit of a trial. The government controls every part of society. Per capita income stands at about $1,500 per year.

There is no limit to what can be done when people have the freedom and opportunity to do better for themselves and their families. That's what hope and a vision can do. The contrast between the two countries might be summed up by the words of Proverbs 29: 18:

"Without a vision, the people perish."

The reverse is also true, with hope and vision people thrive.

And that, dear friends, is why we build memorials, hold parades and give speeches honoring those who have fought for freedom for ourselves and people on distant shores. It is why Veterans Day is a big deal in America.

Hats off to Korean veterans and veterans everywhere who have made enormous sacrifices. You make our world more safe and free so that we may have hope for the future and peace in the present.

Whom Shall We Thank This Thanksgiving?

This fall we stood on the tip of Cape Cod on a wet, cold day and watched the Mayflower II bob offshore. We also peered over a railing at Plymouth Rock, where the Pilgrims first stepped ashore. The day we were there, a Northeaster was blowing hard, rocking everything, so we didn't stay long.

The Pilgrims probably experienced the same type of weather. They arrived at Plymouth on November 21, 1620, after spending 63 storm-tossed days in the hold of a cargo ship. They faced a bitter winter. There was no warm hotel room awaiting them at the end of their journey.

That first winter, about half the 102 Pilgrims died of cold, disease and starvation. But they also found Native American friends, such as the English speaking Squanto, who taught them how to survive in the new land. The next year, in November 1621, they held the first Thanksgiving feast. Their good neighbors were the honored guests at the three-day celebration.

It is popular today to take a jaded view of the Pilgrims and point out their shortcomings. However, it was Theodore Roosevelt who said it's not the critic who counts, but the man in the arena. They had faced so much persecution that they willingly endured the hardships.

Still, the critics are rewriting the history books to avoid the real reasons the Pilgrims came to America.

However, their true objectives are clearly found in the Mayflower Compact, the first governing document of Plymouth Colony.

The Mayflower Compact is just four sentences long. The Pilgrims wrote it on the boat before they went ashore. Yet, it has provided direction for this country for almost 400 years; The U.S. Constitution was based on the general principles found in it:

In the name of God, Amen. We, whose names are underwritten, the loyal subjects of our dread Sovereign Lord King James, by the Grace of God, of Great Britain, France, and Ireland, King, defender of the Faith, etc.

Having undertaken, for the Glory of God, and advancements of the Christian faith and honor of our King and Country, a voyage to plant the first colony in the Northern parts of Virginia, do by these presents, solemnly and mutually, in the presence of God, and one another, covenant and combine ourselves together into a civil body politic; for our better ordering, and preservation and furtherance of the ends aforesaid; and by virtue hereof to enact, constitute, and frame, such just and equal laws, ordinances, acts, constitutions, and offices, from time to time, as shall be thought most meet and convenient for the general good of the colony; unto which we promise all due submission and obedience.

In witness whereof we have hereunto subscribed our names at Cape Cod the 11th of November, in the year of the reign of our Sovereign Lord King James, of England, France, and Ireland, the eighteenth, and of Scotland the fifty-fourth, 1620.

This Thanksgiving, we would do well to remember the beginning of our great nation. America remains a beacon of light to the rest of the world. Let's shrug off the pride we take in our own accomplishments and humbly give God the glory for what he has accomplished through us, the U.S.

There are a number of good books on the topic of Early America. *The Light and the Glory* by Peter Marshall and David Manuel, which was first published in 1977, is an enlightening read and is available online.

The Bittersweet Irony of Thanksgiving

The bittersweet irony of Thanksgiving is once again upon our family. Four members of my immediate family have died in November, two of my sisters, Mary Jean and Donna, died on Thanksgiving Day. Another sister, Evie, and my dad died a few days before Thanksgiving.

My husband's side is not immune, either. His sister and brother-in-law died a few years apart at Thanksgiving.

This, in a season when we give thanks for all our blessings and begin the rush to Christmas joy. Instead of being full of thanks, at times my heart has instead resembled the crusted leftovers at the bottom of the dressing pan.

If ever a person needs favor and grace, it's when life has delivered you to the dark precipice and pushed you into the valley below.

I know a lot about being thankful, learning the phrase "Praise the Lord anyway!" early in my Christian walk. It was easy then, when the world seemed fresh and alive and new. But during times of deep grief, when I passed through the valley of death, my praise well was empty. Indeed, I didn't walk through the valley in my own power, but seemed to be carried by the pallbearers of my grieving spirit.

The death of loved ones is never easy, but the gaping hole left in holidays you once shared is particularly hard to fill. Especially when the deaths cluster together. A cloud hung over me as the years passed. Every Thanksgiving I frantically tried to cover the hole left by absent family members. It wasn't until many years later that I was set free from the oppressive grief and was able to enjoy Thanksgiving again.

Most of those deaths happened many years ago. Then in 2012, as I put the turkey in the oven about dawn on Thanksgiving morning, the phone rang. My oldest sister, Mary Jean, had died a few minutes earlier. Would I sink under the grief again? While her death was not unexpected, it was Thanksgiving. One more Thanksgiving, one more death in the family.

I'm happy to report that year I did not fall into a pit of grief and despair again. The pallbearers of my spirit did their job and carried me through the valley.

Many people experience grief during the holidays. Every year they, and maybe you, face the holidays with a splintered family.

It has now been three decades since the Thanksgiving death pall began in our family. One of the benefits of getting older is you have the perspective of time. For those of you who are grieving during the holidays, here are a few thoughts to hang onto. While they can't fix what happened, perhaps you will find comfort in them:

Use this holiday season to count your blessings.

Tell someone your story. People say they want to help, well, they can by listening. Tell you first memory, best memory, worst memory, last memory and everything in between. At a funeral, sometimes tears give way to stories that make you smile. Find those smiley stories.

Write down your memories. This is a great healer, one of the best ways to deal with grief.

Help others. It will release endorphins into your system and help you find peace.

Volunteer to serve a holiday meal at a homeless shelter. Ring the bell for the Salvation Army. One person I know chooses to work on holidays so others can be with their families.

Finally, ask the Lord Jesus to heal your broken heart and to give you a future and a hope. You may not feel like you want to go on, but you are alive and that means you still have a purpose to fulfill here on earth.

One definition of pall is "the white cloth given in baptism and the resurrection of Christ at Easter." So "pall-bearer" signifies the one who bears a coffin covered by hope of the resurrection. You see, grief has always been associated with grace. It is only through the death and resurrection of Christ that we can have hope for eternal life and hope of seeing our loved ones again.

Isaiah 53: 4 states, "Surely he has borne our griefs and carried our sorrows."

That isn't just a vague promise, but a powerful one. He can and will carry you through the valley of grief and bring you out the other side if you ask him.

Nothing to Fear
this Christmas

Christmas 2015 is de ja vu all over again. Just like the first Christmas, terror, political unrest, and refugees are the hallmarks of the season. The Prince of Peace was born in troubled times, not much different than today. Rome ruled the western world with a brutal hand, causing people to live under a black cloud of fear. In Israel, people divided into political factions seeking freedom from their oppressors.

The tension was ratcheted so high that, based on a rumor, King Herod ordered the murder of all the baby boys in Israel. The young Hebrew family we know as Mary and Joseph, sought asylum in a foreign country to protect their little boy, Jesus.

Like today, people 2,000 years ago put their hope in politics rather than in spiritual renewal. They wanted a military messiah that would throw out the Romans. They weren't prepared for Jesus's message of repentance, hope and peace. I Corinthians I: 27 states that God chose the foolish things of the world to confound the wise. What could be more foolish than sending the Messiah to earth as a baby to be raised by a carpenter in an obscure country?

Yet, across time, no person has had more influence than Jesus. He has changed hearts and fixed broken lives, and thereby has changed nations and the path of history. The good news he brought still uplifts and transforms today as it did when he preached it on a Judean hillside.

This Christmas is a good time to focus on Christ's message. He still offers power for life today, peace amid the chaos offered by the world, and hope for eternity. There will always be trouble in the world, but with his help we can find peace no matter what the circumstance.

One way to do that is to read his book, the Bible, the best-selling book in history! Did you know there are over 3,000 promises in the bible? For the last six months, our Sunday school class has been studying *One Hundred Promises of God* by Nick Harrison. It has helped me more easily see those promises. Here are a couple I really like:

> *"Fear not for I have redeemed you; I have called you by your name; You are mine." That's Isaiah 43: 1.*

> How about this, *"God shall supply all your needs according to his riches in glory by Christ Jesus." Philippians 4: 19.*

In addition, did you know there are over 2,500 prophecies in the bible? The prophet Isaiah lived about 700 years before Christ, yet said this about Jesus in Isaiah 9: 6:

> *"For to us a child is born, to us a son is given, and the government will be on his shoulders. And he will be called Wonderful Counselor, Mighty God, Everlasting Father, Prince of Peace."*

As our pastor, Dan Kent, said recently, "No Jesus, No peace. Know Jesus, know peace." My prayer for you this holiday season is that you will know the peace that Christ brings, because he is still the Prince of Peace.

The Writer

Childhood Dreams

For most of my life, being a writer was an elusive dream. Still, I kept trying. At age eight, I began writing poems. Most of them were melodramatic. One line I particularly remember is, "My mother works hard, she makes lard." That cracked up my mother and sister when they found the notebook and peeked in it.

I'm proud to say that by sixth grade, I wrote well enough to get an "F" on a book report. Each week we wrote reports on books that we'd read. They were put into construction paper bookworms and tacked to the bulletin board. I had done my finest writing and fully expected to get a high grade on it. So when I got a "F" I went to my teacher and asked why.

"You copied it out of the front of the book!" she declared.

But I had written the report myself. She promised to change my grade if I brought her the book to prove it. I had returned the book to the Library, which was only open a few hours a week. A blizzard kept it closed the next day. Then I got the mumps and missed several days of school. Finally, I just accepted the "F". Still, it occurred to me that I wrote well enough to fool my teacher.

At age 13, I wrote sweet and tragic stories about teenage girls in spiral-bound notebooks. My friend, Cindy, thought I should show them to her cousin who was a couple years older and a sophisticated reader. I was excited and nervous to have her read my stories.

The cousin arrived from out of town one bitter cold day. After school Cindy ran home, got her cousin and we all walked to my house. I was already nervous in the presence of this 16-year-old literary critic, although I didn't yet have a clue to what humiliation was about to occur.

I opened the door to our house and got whapped in the face by a pair of long underwear! My mother had washed clothes that day, and she'd strung a clothesline across the dining room to dry underwear and shirts. I was so embarrassed I wanted the floorboards to open up and let me fall through. That ended my teenage writing career for about a year.

When I was a senior in high school, a new young English teacher move to town. We all adored him. He was just a few years older than we were and he was radical. We'd been reading literature and diagraming sentences for years. He decided to put our skills to work and have us write.

He liked an essay that I wrote on the theme of "Yesterday" which was also a popular Beatles song. In fact, he wanted to help me get a scholarship for college. However, I had other plans. Instead of going to college, I married Larry and he went to college. Five years, seven moves and two kids later, we settle in south Bismarck, and I began to think about writing again.

Post script. All of my adult life I wanted to thank Mr. Erickson. I didn't find him until fifty years later. We met up at a café in Phoenix and had a wonderful talk.

I've often thought about what an influence teachers can be and how seldom they see the results of their hard work and dedication. So, please let those special teachers in your life know that they made a difference.

Lessons from the Creek

When I was about six, I tried to cross Cottonwood Creek by leaping from stone to stone. I made it to the other side, but my shoes and anklets were wet. That's how I feel about the last year as I've gotten my feet wet as a published author.

Yes, a year ago this month, the UPS guy rang the doorbell and left two boxes of books on our steps. The first copies of By the Banks of Cottonwood Creek had arrived...a week early. I've been trying to catch up ever since!

My first book signing was arranged for just two days later. The following Sunday, I signed books at a craft show in Braddock, N.D. (pop. 21). When we arrived home, a stranger had left a phone message saying she'd purchased the book. She was enjoying reading it and wanted to know if I had other books out. (Note: What a dear fan, she's purchased every book since then.)

That got to be a theme. People who liked the book at all, really loved it. They read it fast and wanted a sequel right away. Could I write another book?

But I was busy marketing "Cottonwood Creek" and writing a historical novel. Wasn't that enough? I had over eight years and my heart invested in my historical novel, so I began working extra hard on it to finish it. Then one euphoric day, after a marathon writing session, it was finished. Oh my beloved historical novel, may you find a publisher soon!

Meanwhile, I started writing the sequel to "Cottonwood Creek" and am really into it. In fact, I've received a few odd looks this year when I talk about the characters as if they are real people. They are to me! They live in my head making decisions, talking to each other, proposing marriage...

Leaping among the creek-washed stones this year, I've learned a lot. Chiefly, that it is God who helps me show life on the prairie and how people can live, love and work with Him at the center of their lives.

In a recent rerun of the British sitcom Downton Abbey, the cook, Mrs. Patmore, was going blind. She was afraid to admit it, because as she put it, "What use is a blind cook?" When she was brought into the presence of her employer, Lord Grantham, she expected to be fired. Instead, he arranged for her to have eye surgery in London, so she could continue as a valued part of the household.

That's how I feel. I have so many shortcomings and blind spots, but the Lord brings me into his presence and lets me know I'm valued. There are so many scriptures that encourage me, but none more than in the book of Philippians. Consider these words:

> *"Being confident of this very thing, that He who has begun a good work in you will complete it..." Phil. 1: 6*

> *"I press toward the goal for the prize of the upward call of God in Christ Jesus." Phil. 3: 14*

> *"I can do all things through Christ who strengthens me." Phil. 4: 13*

The outpouring of good will from friends and readers also inspires me. Thank you for your kind words, giving editorial feedback, and encouraging me when my doubts and fears creep in. Thank you for purchasing books, providing publicity, stocking the book in your shop, and hosting book signings or readings. I'm grateful to people who pray for me daily. I feel the power of those prayers! I'm especially grateful to Larry, who agreeably waded into this adventure with me. Thank you and God bless you every one.

Living the Dream

My "publicity tour" may have peaked last week. A radio interview, book reading and book signing were enough glamour for this prairie chick. New York television interviews will have to wait.

At one point, I lounged on a kitchen stool and listened to my radio interview being rebroadcast on KNDR, complete with book giveaway. I said to my husband, "Wow! We're living the dream!" That was Wednesday.

Those summit moments are rare and must be treasured. Reality lives between them.

The evening before the radio interview, when I planned to prepare for it, I instead became a Refrigerator Repair Assistant. An ominous drip had developed in the fridge, so my handy husband pushed it to the middle of the kitchen and cleaned the coils with the vacuum. My job was to turn the vacuum on and off, on and off. It took the better part of the evening.

Thursday I was back in the dream. I did a Book Read at Touchmark Retirement Center. I read a few portions of *By the Banks of Cottonwood Creek*. (Since it was a hot day, I read part of the snowstorm chapter.) The audience asked questions and I signed some copies of the book. It was a feel-good moment in time: A lovely setting in the chapel. A respectable audience of readers and writers from the community, as well as Touchmark residents.

I hugged that moment for the rest of the week as I continued to "live the dream."

It's not all glamour, I told myself as I drove to K-Mart in 98-degree heat on Friday. I needed a couple bags of Tootsie Rolls for a book signing at Huntington Books in Mandan on Saturday.

The plan was to be in front of the bookstore under a canopy for a couple hours. The Wild West Rib Fest would be in full swing just up the street. With throngs of people moving up and down the sidewalk, I even wondered if I should bring an extra supply of books.

It was hot on Saturday. So hot the chefs at the grill fest probably turned off their grills and let the meat sizzle in the sun. The temperature hovered at 105 degrees for hours. The book signing was moved into the tiny air-conditioned shop entry so I wouldn't melt like a deserted ice cream cone. Traffic disappeared. People were probably sprawled in the coolest level of their houses remembering how a few months earlier they'd yearned for summer.

In wrapping up this post, a couple things happened: I had first included a Will Rogers quote: "Why not go out on a limb? That's where all the best fruit is." Last evening I decided to delete it. I shut down the computer and picked up my devotional. The reading for the day was headlined "Risk your life and get more than you ever dreamed," a paraphrase of Luke 19: 26 in The Message. A few lines down was a challenge: "If you want 'more than you ever dreamed,' you've got to go out on a limb. That's where the best fruit is."

What are the chances of coming across that same quote again?

The second irony happened this morning. As regular readers know, I get my morning attitude adjustment from the comic page of the Bismarck Tribune. This morning the *Zits* teenage character is "living the dream"! He finally got a job at a supermarket. He is hoping to be promoted to smashing melons into a dumpster. Ah, we each have our own dreams, don't we?

I can't help but feel there is a reader or two out there who needs to begin living their dream, whether it be writing the great American novel or smashing melons. So, dear readers, is there a dream burning in your heart? If so, why not seek the Lord's direction and then begin the journey?

A Light for My Path

These days, every time the doorbell rings I hope the first copies of Secrets of the Dark Closet have arrived. Anticipation is high. Is the cover appealing? Will anyone read it? Will they like it?

Soon I'll see the results of the road I've taken.

At the same time, I keep finding quotes about paths and roads, like this one that surfaced this morning: *He will turn troubles into highways*—Catherine Marshall.

Or this one by Robert Frost that Pastor Dan quoted last Sunday: *Two roads diverged in a wood, and I—I took the one less traveled by, And that has made all the difference.*

Writing is a little like traveling a wooded road, because you can't see very far in front of you. Back in the 1980s when my uncle, Wallace Muir, began researching the family history, no one suspected his path would lead to the door of Gram's dark closet.

Uncle Wally wanted to do the genealogy, and lay to rest some rumors that had hovered around the family. He spent more than 20 years on the project. I was fascinated as, one by one, he dug out and documented scandalous facts. But little did I know I'd be compelled to write about my sweet grandmother, Bessie Kloubec Muir, who took so many secrets to her grave.

"The Muir-Kloubec Genealogy and History 1708-2005" was finally published in 2005. Uncle Wally was a good writer and he added many anecdotes to the family history, but the data he included overwhelmed the human story.

When he died three years later (at the age of 87), I inherited 93 pounds of his records. Sifting through census records, letters, early genealogies and other documents he had collected, I tried to imagine what Bessie did, said, and thought. After all, she was only 11 when her family came apart at the seams.

Here is the question that I believe troubled Bessie during her growing up years: *"A person goes through life making one choice after another. How can you tell if a choice will take you down a road you do not want to go?"*

During the years of writing, I asked myself similar questions. Was it worth it to spend so much time writing her story? Would she want her "dirty laundry" aired? Was using real names the right thing to do?

Psalm 119: 105 states: "Thy word is a lamp for my feet, a light for my path."

When I read that, my mind's eye sees a well-lit, paved street stretching into the distance. But in reality, my own journey seems more like Frost's path through a dark woods. Maybe that's the way it's supposed to be. Maybe we aren't given detailed itineraries for our lives so we learn to develop faith and courage. I often sought God for direction. Doing the following things helped me feel sure I was on the right road. They can help you, too:

Read the Bible every day. It is still the most reliable place to go for answers.

Get over my independence and ask for guidance. Have you ever found yourself driving around the same block looking for an address? The Lord has better answers than Alexa. Let your requests be known.

Be guided by peace. When we are on the right road, the peace of God settles on us, no matter what our circumstances.

Outwardly, it seemed foolish to write *Secrets of the Dark Closet,* but after seeking God, I still felt compelled in that direction. Not until I finished the last page, in a blazing memorable moment, did I begin to understand the power of Bessie's story.

Recently I was thrilled to receive a letter from my high school English teacher. He was the first person to fuel my desire to write. Now, decades later, he is still the epitome of encouragement and graceful writing. One phrase of his letter really struck me. He said, *"God...pieces together the wonderful tapestry of our event-filled lives to give them both temporal and eternal meaning."*

Through the writing process, I've come to believe that the landscape of our families is stitched into our hearts in ways we cannot fathom. The journey of my family includes the riveting story of a young girl named Bessie. It's time to shine a light on her path.

Hometown Jitters

Growing up in LaMoure, my friends and I found many excuses to walk uptown after school. The little treks provided much-needed breaks between the end of the school day and the beginning of homework.

Every week we'd go to the library to return books and check out something new with our library cards. Sometimes we stopped at the Post Office to send a letter to a pen pal or to get the mail.

If we had spare money, we might visit Elmer's Bakery for a maple-frosted long-john or the Dairy Bar for a nickel ice cream cone. Some of our classmates lived over or behind their family's businesses, so it wasn't unusual to stop at Gabe's Grocery or the LaMoure Hotel. The most intriguing store was Sivertson's Variety, worthy of its own story someday. A swing through Rickford's Federated Store was a must to see the latest in shoes and fabric.

Inevitably, we ended up at the LaMoure Drug Store where we purchased school supplies, birthday presents and other schoolgirl necessities, like makeup.

Not once in those years, did I ever dream the LaMoure Drug Store would someday carry a book by me. But yesterday I called to inquire whether they would be interested and they said yes!

Now I have the jitters, because by this time next week By the Banks of Cottonwood Creek will be on the shelf in my hometown.

Publishing your writing is like being in first grade and holding up your art project for your classmates to judge. It's like standing on stage for the first time during amateur hour, before an audience full of expressionless North Dakotans. It's like holding up your newborn baby for the world; the baby looks like you, but you hope people will think he or she is cute, anyway.

At least I feel that vulnerable as a new author. Writing is so very personal. *By the Banks of Cottonwood Creek* isn't about me or my hometown. Still, what is in the book is the sum total of a million of my own personal hopes, thoughts, insights and experiences. For instance, the description of the creek found in the Epilogue is true. I've seen the marshy place where it begins and know the kind of life it supports, but I put the creek in a fictional community.

So, you might ask, why bother publishing if it leaves me feeling vulnerable? The answer can be found in Romans 5: 5. That scripture states: "Now hope does not disappoint, because the love of God has been poured out in our hearts by the Holy Spirit who was given to us."

How I love the scriptures about hope and how it never fails. *By the Banks of Cottonwood Creek* is about hope, about second chances and about finding the future with the help of God. If ever there was a time when people needed that steadying word, it is now.

Emily Dickinson said it this way: "Hope is the thing with feathers – that perches in the soul – and sings the tune without words – and never stops at all." I love the first stanza of that poem and, of course, I like the second one where she mentions me by name: "And sweetest – in the Gale is heard – and sore must be the storm – that could abash the little bird – that kept so many warm."

Have a hope-filled week. Take a stroll down Main Street. And keep searching for the good, a word spelled so much like "God."

The "Rich" Life
of an Author

Some people may think an author's life is all glamour. That's because they haven't seen the author doing back stretches after sitting at the computer all day or lugging her books into a venue to sell. Another delusion is that being a published author makes a person rich. I'm still waiting for that ship to come in.

Meanwhile, I am rich in wonderful experiences. Let me share what happened one afternoon last month when I spoke at a local assisted living and basic care home.

I was warned in advance that the audience wasn't likely to buy any books, so instead of talking about my new book, *Cottonwood Dreams*, I told them about writing *Secrets of the Dark Closet*. Since *Secrets* was published four years ago, I've learned that the topic has universal appeal. Apparently, every family has its secrets.

After putting in a fair amount of time preparing the talk, I drove a few blocks to the home. Once there, I was dismayed to see most of the audience was in wheelchairs and several were asleep!

"It takes a moment to judge someone, but a lifetime to understand them." – Tina Ng

Soon after I began, it became clear that looks were deceiving. Several people smiled or nodded as I talked. When I asked questions, they were eager to share stories. A young fellow sitting in a wheelchair at the back of the room took photos for me.

One woman was so bent over, her head was almost on her lap and one leg was all wrapped up. From time to time, she would raise up and nod at me. That tugged at my heart strings! Later, I sat with her and learned she's in her late 90s. We had a rich conversation about family secrets and the times we live in.

When I was about to leave, there was a ruckus in the hall. After the talk, one lady had wheeled her chair through the building, taken the elevator to her room, and was dashing back. I heard her call out, "Is she still here? Can I still buy a book?"

That was my one sale for the day, and though it was only $12, it was priceless.

Here's another story. I went to the KNDR-FM studio to do a live radio interview mid-September. At 8 a.m. I usually haven't muttered the word "coffee" by that time. Sigh.

Three days later at the Northbrook Mall Vendor Show, I learned the "sacrifice" was worth it. The first person who stopped by my table had heard the interview. She'd driven over 60 miles to see me and arrived as the doors opened. The second person was also from out of town. She stopped by to say thank you because she'd won the book giveaway on KNDR.

Later, another woman expressed a curious interest in the Prairie Pastor Series, and then she really surprised me. She'd read the first two books and *she guessed the name of the little country church on which Cottonwood Church is modeled.* That delighted me, and even more so after learning that she grew up attending that church.

Lately, these wonderful encounters have been happening almost every week, and this author is feeling rich indeed.

"The best and most beautiful things in the world cannot be seen or even touched - they must be felt with the heart." Helen Keller

Great Houses
of Inspiration

This past summer we were privileged to tour Jack London's home near Glen Ellen, California. His great-niece, a former schoolteacher and friend of my niece, gave the private tour.

London owned 1,400 acres in the Valley of the Moon. Visitors can see the foundation of Wolf House, the 15,000 square foot mansion he built, although it burned down before he could move into it. You wouldn't want to miss the House of Happy Walls Museum, a stone mansion built by his wife Charmian after his death. There are also vineyards, redwood, and outbuildings to see on the grounds.

My favorite place was London's writing cottage, a place where he retreated to write his best sellers, such as *Call of the Wild, White Fang, The Sea Wolf,* and *In the Valley of the Moon.*

The building was styled similar to other houses in the early 20th century. The cottage was their private retreat. London wrote in a large study filled with books and tables where he and Charmian spent a lot of time.

He also liked to write a sleeping porch. Windows and wainscot walls, a narrow bed and a desk. That's about all of the furnishings. But it looked out on a beautiful garden and Sonoma Mountain in the distance. It was easy to see why London liked to write in the porch. It is said he often slept there after writing long, erratic hours.

London lived from 1876 to 1916, only forty years. He lived hard and associated with the leaders of his time. He was a vagabond, war correspondent, farmer and writer. This peek into the life of this intelligent, troubled man was the most heart-touching.

I like architecture and am interested in how other writers live, what inspires them, and their writing techniques. So, visiting the homes of authors is a natural.

Another home we have visited that is very different from London's is the Charles and Caroline Ingalls home in DeSmet, S.D.

Laura Ingalls Wilder didn't actually live in the Ingalls home because she was already married when Pa finished building it in 1889. However, she certainly would have spent a lot of time there.

The two-story white frame house was memorable to me because it is eerily like the one in which I lived in while growing up. The porch had two doors leading into the house exactly like ours. The front door opened to the dining room. A partition was built in their dining room so Laura's sister Mary, who was blind, could have a room on the first floor.

All of the rooms were in the same places as our house, and ironically, many of the furnishings were similar. We have also been to the little cabin in Wisconsin where Laura based her first book, *Little House in the Woods.*

Touring the homes of famous people is always fun. We've been to Abraham Lincoln's lovely home in Springfield, Illinois, and Harry Truman's birthplace in Missouri, which had an outhouse in the backyard near the clothesline. That made me feel that Harry was someone who could related to the average American.

I've seen the homes of Louisa May Alcott and Norman Rockwell out east, and Charles Schultz's Art Center and skating rink out west. In Rhode Island, I toured a "summer cottage" of a wealthy 19th Century baron. It was far grander than the biggest mansions elsewhere. In Dunbar, Scotland, my cousins and I traipsed through John Muir's home and wondered if he was a distant relative.

One of the most historical homes in America is The Old Manse, located in Concord, Mass. We've been there, too. It was built in 1770 by Ralph Waldo Emerson's grandfather, William. Located near the North Bridge, the family witnessed from the windows "the shot heard round the world" that began the Revolutionary War. In addition to generations of Emersons, Nathanial Hawthorne also lived there.

All of these houses are bathed in history and offer insight into bright, creative minds. Yet, to me the most inspirational house is the House of the Lord. I'm not thinking about writing when I'm in church (usually). However, being in church, spending time with the God, and reading his word helps me tap into greater creativity.

Have you ever noticed that you begin to act, sound and think like the people you hang out with? Then it's reasonable to think that reading great books and spending time with great people is inspiring. And at the top of the list is spending time with the Creator of the Universe.

"I was glad when they said to me, "Let us go to the house of the LORD." NLT

The Writers Group

For the past year, I've belonged to a writers group that meets weekly. I started because I needed unbiased eyes to read my material. Seven of us have met regularly since then. Others come and go, depending on their schedules and need for literary help.

There are many types of writers groups. Some are only for one genre, such as fantasy, fiction or non-fiction. Some are for just woman or just men. They may be affiliated with universities or bookstores.

Ours is none of the above. Yesterday the readings were from a couple memoirs, poetry, a western, a violent children's fantasy, an action fantasy and some Christian fiction. Our group, Dakota Writers, was launched several years ago by OLLI, the Osher Lifelong Learning Institute. Today it runs on its own.

Our members are doctors, teachers, social workers, in public relations, and in fast food, along with one bus driver and a cowboy. Most of them are university graduates. In the past year, at least three members have published articles or books.

While writing is solitary work, meeting with the Dakota Writers is noisy. So noisy that we depend on a bell to quiet everyone down and a timer to make sure each person has a chance to read. Sometimes, like a kindergartener, you have to raise your hand to be heard.

The group is not subtle. Unlike kindergarten, you don't get stars for coloring poorly. No, when you've finished reading, everyone talks at once, launching into what is wrong with your format, and pointing out typos, redundant language or the disconnect between page one and two.

I love this group. They challenge and frustrate me at times, but I am thrilled when they have an arresting suggestion or point out a flaw I absolutely couldn't see. My writing is better for having read it aloud to them and for their forthright evaluation.

Reading before the group is a lot like baring your soul, because writing is so very personal. Although I've received my share of "constructive" criticism, one of my best moments came last fall. I had taken the first few pages of my historical novel to them. This manuscript is the essence of my life's work, my baby, part of my soul. (Still unpublished.)

After they had ripped apart the work of a couple previous readers, I was up next. What if they tore apart my beloved first chapter? I thought about tucking the pages in my notebook and leaving. Instead, I found some gumption and began to read aloud. When I finished, there was an unusual hush in the room. It turned out they liked my story! They had minimal suggestions. My spirit soared.

Recently, I was thrilled when several members attended my first Book Reading. I joined the writers group because I needed unbiased eyes to read my work. Since then the members of Dakota Writers have become friends as well.

For information on starting a writer's group, check out the Writer's Digest website at www.writersdigest. com.

A Sneak Peek at Cottonwood Dreams

Spring has sprung, and it's time to look forward to summer fun. Much of my fun takes place in our tiny gardens. The daylilies and roses are peeking through the ground and we have purchased several bags of fertilizer and mulch. It's a season of optimism.

I am also happy because my next book is almost finished. It took 20 months to write *Cottonwood Dreams* and another four months for the editing process. Those are the first two steps in publishing. Next, the manuscript will be sent off to the publisher. Waiting (and wading) through this step can take weeks or months. Then it'll be time to let everyone know it's available and dig out my book-signing pen.

I hope readers will like this book. All of the characters from *By the Banks of Cottonwood Creek* and *Amber's Choice* are in it, but the main characters are Brianna Davis and Tiny Winger.

The truth is I didn't think Brianna was very likable in the other books. She was too tall, too pretty, too successful, and too haughty. Give me someone I can relate to! However, I began to wonder how she felt about being pretty. Did it cause her problems? How did it feel to find success so young? Slowly her story was revealed to me.

I could see her standing in front of Aunt Kate's Queen Anne house in Schulteville, clutching her sewing machine and suitcase. Brianna was dumping her glamorous life and pinning her last hope on the love and friendships she'd found in North Dakota.

Tiny began as a minor character in *By the Banks of Cottonwood Creek*, but he developed a following among readers. Everyone liked this shy hometown guy who wore a greasy cap and oozed common sense. Well, almost everyone liked him. Brianna didn't. And clearly, the feeling was mutual. Then, they were forced to spend time together.

Cottonwood Dreams is the story of Brianna and Tiny's relationship and the good-hearted people that surround them in both their happiest and most difficult moments. It's about faith and friendship helping them navigate life.

It's also about mental illness. Did you know this illness takes many forms? It's misunderstood, difficult to diagnose and devastates families. Tiny has lived under its weight, and Brianna is about to have it thrown in her face.

Writing *Cottonwood Dreams* kept me busy through the long months of Covid-19 isolation. Along the way, I've heard from readers who ask how the writing is going or when the book will be published. Your comments are like Miracle- Gro™ for this writer!

Sometimes, I go through my "kudos" file and say a prayer of thanks for readers that take time to write a note. Knowing you read my book in one sitting, can relate to a character, or found encouragement in the pages means more to me than you can imagine. Thank you.

Now, here is a word of encouragement for *you*: "The Lord himself goes before you and will be with you; he will never leave you nor forsake you. Do not be afraid; do not be discouraged." Deuteronomy 31:8

May you be blessed with sunshine, flowers and the warmth of God's grace this spring.

No Ordinary Day!

Last Saturday was a sunny August day. The drought-parched prairie had received a good rain and the grass seemed to turn green again overnight. This day the windows were open to a summer breeze. I was making a mess in the kitchen, canning corn relish.

It was an ordinary day except for one thing: *Secrets of the Dark Closet* was supposed to be available at any time. And so, mid-afternoon I checked the internet and found my historical novel on Amazon.

Suddenly it was no ordinary day. My second book was published! A mountain summit moment. Behind me lay the peaks and valleys of decades of research, years of writing and editing, and months with the publisher.

Writing is nothing if it isn't a test of perseverance. A.A. Milne, who wrote *Winnie the Pooh,* said, "Rivers know this: there is no hurry. We shall get there some day."

My "someday" was Saturday and I was elated. Still, I'm a prairie girl at heart. Practical. Dutiful. So instead whooping it up with friends and family, I finished canning the relish, and even preserved some sweet cherries. Note: The jars all sealed! There are various definitions of success. As every home ec student and 4-H member knows, success is a sealed jar.

But back to the book. On Monday, things got even better, because Secrets rose to # 20 in the Top 100 New Young Adult Category on Amazon!

Harvey McKay said, "When you have a dream that

you can't let go of, trust your instincts and pursue it. But remember: Real dreams take work, they take patience, and sometimes they require you to dig down very deep. Be sure you're willing to do that."

Publishing *Secrets of the Dark Closet* is that dream for me.

What are your dreams?

Jeremiah 29: 11 states that "For I know the plans I have for you," declares the LORD, "plans to prosper you and not to harm you, plans to give you hope and a future."

Hopes and dreams can bring a sense of purpose and even add years to your life. You may not want to write a book. Instead, you may dream of opening a business, taking up a new hobby, setting a goal for getting healthy, or traveling to a special place in the world.

So what are you waiting for? Perhaps whatever is burning in your heart was put there by God for a special purpose. Talk to him about it, and then step out in faith. Following that dream can turn an ordinary day into a once-in-a-lifetime experience.

"A good friend is a blessing from God." I Samuel 18: 3

Faith
Essays

Hello, this is God Speaking

Does God speak to us? How can we know it's really him and not that double mocha latte we drank?

This winter, my goal was to complete the sequel to *By the Banks of Cottonwood Creek*. That was interrupted by the need to revise the proposal for my *Secrets of the Dark Closet* manuscript. No problem. I had the ambitious (delusional?) idea that I could rewrite the proposal in a week's time and still wrap up the *Cottonwood* sequel before spring. But, when March came and the daffodils poked up, both writing projects were stuck in the mud.

I frantically worked at one and then the other. It became clear that I needed help, but no one could give me direction in how to complete either one. That is when the Lord began to give me guidance. And once again I realized that he is the author and I am the ghost writer.

This month, I began to see a particular message everywhere about how God calls us for his purpose. Now, this fits right in with the subject of the *Cottonwood* sequel, where Amber Rose McLean is struggling with choices related to her marriage and career.

On March 1-4, my devotional was all about God's call on our lives. This booklet often has something relevant to my life. These four days it reflected on John Ortberg's *If You Want to Walk on Water You Have to Get Out of the Boat*. We studied Ortberg's book a few years ago in Sunday school. He is a familiar and credible author. Each day's devotional gave me detailed insight into the direction to take the Cottonwood sequel.

March 5, I went to the Used Book sale at Bismarck Public Library to look for books for the church library. There, a book called *The Call of God* all but waved at me. This was written by Brother Andrew, author of *God's Smuggler* and a 20th century hero of the Christian faith. The first pages were full of insight and encouragement.

That same week, God's calling came up again when some Superbook DVDs came in the mail for the children's collection at the church library. The first to arrive was Samuel and *The Call of God*. Hmm. Then, I began stumbling over the word "calling" in my daily bible reading, such as this verse: "(May) the eyes of your understanding being enlightened; that you may know what is the hope of His calling..." Ephesians 1: 18, NKJ. Yeah, he was enlightening me all right.

Maybe like me, you wonder when God is speaking to your heart and when you should avoid the mocha lattes for a while. Here are some ways to figure that out: The message will always line up with God's word. It will be confirmed in more than one way. The sources will be credible. The peace of Christ will be in the message.

When I listen for God's voice and follow his leading, my life calms down and writing becomes much easier. It makes me think of these words from an old hymn, "Tenderly, softly Jesus is calling, calling for you and for me...come home, come home, all who are weary, come home."

Finding the Favor of God

e were driving home after a trip out west. At dusk, we stopped in a Wyoming town and asked a gas station attendant about a good place to stay. She said her friend owned a "nice" motel just a couple blocks away. Beyond tired, we took her advice and stopped there for the night.

Worst. Motel. Experience. Ever. The shabby little motel sat a stone's throw from a railroad track and coal trains rumbled past about every fifteen minutes. The whole room juddered so badly that the dust fell from the curtains like snowflakes and the lone picture rattled against the wall. We hardly got any sleep.

The next morning, we left and drove over a hill not a mile away. And there, there in the early morning sunlight, sat a mirage: A lovely hotel/convention center with an iridescent fountain in the front acreage. Swans floated gracefully on a lake. Flowers grew profusely.

For an instant, we thought maybe one of those trains had gone off the track, and we had died and were rolling into heaven. But no, we were in still in Wyoming. We stopped to eat breakfast in this beautiful setting. It turned out that a room at the nice place cost about the same as at the Locomotive Motel.

So often we settle for less, when something so much better is within reach.

Finding and living in the favor of God is one of those things we can miss entirely and never know it, just as we missed the nice place to stay because we didn't believe we had a better choice.

But what exactly is favor? One of my favorite definitions is "gracious kindness."

Recently, my sister-in-law, Dee Dee, served as a very human example of gracious kindness. She wants the very best for her granddaughter, so when the little girl celebrated her fifth birthday, Grandma bought dozens of delightful gifts for her. She stayed up late wrapping presents and could hardly wait for her granddaughter to open them.

Dee Dee enjoys giving good gifts, she has the means to give them and she loves her granddaughter enough to want the best for her. All her granddaughter has to do is open the gifts. She doesn't have to earn them, they are hers because she's part of the family.

The same can be said of God. He enjoys giving his children good gifts, he has the means to do it, and he wants the very best for us. Our part is to receive his gifts. Jesus himself said, *"If you, then, though you are evil, know how to give good gifts to your children, how much more will your Father in heaven give good gifts to those who ask Him?"*

What gifts does he have for us? Wow! The list is long, but it starts with the gift of eternal life, made possible through great sacrifice. How about peace of mind? Joy in the midst of trials? Healing for our hearts and bodies? Favor with God and humankind?

When my husband and I were newbie Christians, we heard Bob Buess speak on the favor of God. He said, *"Your success and favor do not depend on your intelligence or ignorance, or your strength or weakness. Rather, they depend on your absolute conviction that your victory is in Jesus Christ and not in yourself."*

Too often, I forge ahead on my own and end up in an unpleasant place, rather than seeking out the help and blessing of my heavenly Father. But that doesn't mean that he isn't there, beckoning me to his knee, ready to favor me with love and kindness. Ready to favor you, too, because he is *"able to do immeasurably more than all we ask or imagine, according to his power that is at work within us."*

Hidden Treasures

The faded red barn on our farm was the center of activity when I was growing up. Each morning and evening the cows filed into the stanchions to be milked. Noisy calves, pigs or sheep were housed on the north side. The horses had the best stall of all, right by the door. When my dad wasn't in a rush to get the crops planted or the harvest in, he still liked to use his team of horses, Trix and Tony, for fieldwork.

The second floor of the barn held the hayloft. Hay was lifted through a giant door at the front and stored for winter use. Later it was pushed out that same door into a hayrack to feed the cattle in the barnyard.

To get to the hayloft, you had to climb a set of boards nailed to the wall inside the barn. I remember working up my courage to climb that ladder for the first time, but soon I easily scrambled up it. I loved to play all year round in the fragrant alfalfa stored in the haymow. However, spring was especially fun, because our mother cat liked to raise her kittens in the warm, quiet loft.

If I discovered the kittens before their eyes were open, I had to wait for a few days until I could pick them up. They were much too delicate to be handled by a little girl's hands. However, once they were old enough to play, I'd visit them several times a day.

Finding those kittens was like finding hidden treasure. Each day I delighted in watching them grow up. First, they nestled with their mother, then they began wobbling from their cozy hollow. Before long, they were chasing the dust motes that gleamed in the sunlight streaming through a high window. Once they began pouncing on and wrestling with each other, I knew they would soon travel beyond the haymow.

For a prairie girl living on a farm with no other children nearby, the kittens were indeed hidden treasures. Finding them brought a lot of happiness to my life.

Today, I wouldn't mind finding a nest of kittens once again, but I can count on finding another hidden treasure every day. There are many hidden gems for us in the Bible. Made up of 66 books, written by 40 authors, over 1,500 years, it contains history, adventure, prophecy, hope and encouragement.

Even when we are very familiar with the Bible, passages can leap out at us and give us new understanding to apply to our lives. The advice found there is better than any self-help book.

There are versions of the Bible for every reading preference. I personally like those with modern language, such as the New King James or The Living Bible. They are much easier to understand than texts with older language. If you haven't read the Bible in some time, a trip through the gospel of Mark or John is a good place to start.

Colossians 3: 16 states "Let the word of Christ richly dwell within you." That's the New American Standard, by the way. Finding that richness is way more valuable than finding a batch of kittens and just as exciting.

In the Garden

s I write this, we're between Mother's Day and Memorial Day, two holidays infused with flowers, music, and nostalgia. For me, May is also the launch of garden season. Our garden includes a small square behind the house and numerous pots filled with flowers and vegetables. We enjoy nurturing them all summer.

"A garden is predictable. The melody has already been written, or at least the chord progression," Richard Brookhiser recently wrote in the National Review.

I hadn't thought of gardens as being predictable. After all, you never know what kind of crop you're going to get. Still, we believe (predict, hope) seeds and baby plants will grow up to be beautiful, fragrant flowers or tasty, bountiful vegetables.

A best-loved hymn is about gardens. C. Austin Miles wrote In the Garden in his basement with no garden in sight. Instead, he saw a vision of Mary at the empty tomb as described in John 20:14. The words came to him in a rush. That evening he set them to music. Here are the words:

I come to the garden alone While the dew is still on the roses And the voice I hear, falling on my ear The son of God discloses.

He speaks and the sound of His voice is so sweet, the birds hush their singing, And the melody that He gave to me With in my heart is ringing.

I'd stay in the garden with Him Though the night around me is falling But He bids me go

Through the voice of woe His voice to me is calling.

And He walks with me And He talks with me And He tells me I am His own And the joy we share as we tarry there None other has ever known. C. Austin Miles

When I was a new Christian, I preferred contemporary Christian music to hymns. I didn't know that when In the Garden was written in 1912, it was modern Christian music. It also went against tradition by describing a sweet personal friendship with Jesus, rather than seeing him as an unapproachable God.

Today, I love this hymn. It has even more meaning in this interlude between Mother's Day and Memorial Day because it was sung at my mother's funeral, as well as my three sisters' funerals. They were all gardeners. I like to think they're now enjoying a heavenly garden.

While, some of the most important events in the Bible took place in the Garden of Eden and the Garden of Gethsemane, Revelations 22:1-2 shows that there are gardens in heaven, too:

"Then the angel showed me the river of the water of life, as clear as crystal, flowing from the throne of God and of the Lamb down the middle of the great street of the city. On each side of the river stood the tree of life, bearing twelve crops of fruit, yielding its fruit every month. And the leaves of the tree are for the healing of the nations."

This May season is the perfect time to enjoy a quiet interlude in a garden, park or other pretty spot. While there, let us listen for his sweet voice and be open to his friendship.

"Kiss of the sun for pardon. Song of the birds for mirth. You're closer to God's heart in a garden Than any place on earth." – Dorothy Frances Gurney

I Can Only Imagine

As much as we joke about going to Boot Hill someday or tell stories about St. Peter guarding the gates of heaven, when death comes for a loved one, it's no laughing matter.

It's been a long winter for our family. We've had a series of deaths on both sides of the family. The slippery slope of declining health had already changed family dynamics. It's been years since we all packed up our kids and went to the river for a day of grilled burgers and raucous water fights. It's even been a long time since we've spent a big, noisy Christmas together.

With each goodbye, we try to imagine what happens when we die. Is heaven real? Are our loved ones there? Will we go to heaven? The answer to these questions is found in the Easter story.

Easter is the most important and oldest festival of the Christian Church, celebrating the resurrection of Jesus Christ. It separates Christianity from every other religion. Other beliefs teach that we must work our way to heaven, but Christians believe Jesus did the work for us.

Sadly, many people believe in God and try to lead good lives, but they miss this truth. They don't know where they will spend eternity. But we can know, and when we understand what Jesus did for us, that truth will fills us with hope and joy!

This month, a fine man and great evangelist died. Billy Graham shared one message throughout his career, what Jesus said in John 3: 16: "For God so loved the world that he gave his one and only Son, that whoever believes in him shall not perish but have eternal life."

It's that simple:

Believe that Jesus carried our sins to the cross.

Humbly admit that you can't save yourself.

Accept his free gift of salvation.

The Lenten days leading up to Easter are a wonderful time for soul searching. We clean our houses in anticipation of the holiday. Why not also get rid of our lingering doubts about what happens when we die? Take God's Word to heart.

The movie, "I Can Only Imagine" is a very powerful true story of singer songwriter Bart Millard of the MercyMe band. The movie had me gripping the arm of my seat, stuffing back tears, as well as laughing.

The movie is based on the song "I Can Only Imagine," the best-selling Christian song of all time. Perhaps it's so popular because in it Millard envisions what heaven will be like. The movie and song are both infused with the hope and truth we need so badly in this old world.

So, let's take a step of faith and believe that Jesus paid the price for us to spend eternity in heaven. It's that simple. And then we will find the joy that Jesus's followers had on that first Easter Morning. With them, we will can say, He is Risen! He has Risen Indeed!

The Path to Peace

Where can you find a Catholic priest, a Black grandmother and a Messianic Jew dancing together? The answer is important today with the racial tension that has seized our beloved America, pitting us against each other. Agitators want to stir us up and make us angry with people of other races or beliefs.

But there is another way. We can live in peace with each other. Not an uneasy peace or surface tolerance, but living with true brotherly love.

I was privileged to attend the 1977 Conference on Charismatic Renewal in the Christian Churches in Kansas City. The conference took place in the midst of a spiritual renewal that swept the world beginning in the 1960s.

My journey toward Kansas City actually began four years earlier. I had always believed in God, but he seemed very distant, and Jesus was just a historical figure to me. And then I learned through my mother-in-law that *Jesus was alive!* My life turned around as I learned more about Jesus.

Part of my journey included attending a weekly prayer meeting at Corpus Christi Church, where people of many denominations gathered to praise and worship the Lord. Some of my husband's family attended similar meetings in Aberdeen. The way opened for us all to go to the Kansas City conference.

A chartered bus picked up a delegation from Bismarck, and then made stops along Interstate 94, where others waited to board with suitcases and big smiles. At Aberdeen, we picked up the largest group of people. It was such a happy crowd. A young brother from the monastery at Richardton led singing all the way down. We must have sung *The Lord is a Great and Mighty King* at least 50 times each way!

That happy beginning continued for the next five days. Once in KC, there were hundreds of teaching sessions to choose from during the day. Then in the evening about 50,000 people gathered at the Royals stadium.

This prairie girl had never seen so many people in one place, let alone so many people worshipping God with all of their hearts. I saw a Black women, who worshipped with tambourines next to Messianic Jews with their long beards, who worshipped Yeshua, another name for Jesus. We were all one in the Lord that week.

Our joy spilled over on all of Kansas City. And the world noted it. Headlines in the Kansas City Times read: "City Enjoying Biggest, Cleanest, Happiest Rally" and "Stadium Resounds With Praise." The conference made the headlines from New York to Miami to Los Angeles.

To praise God is to invite his presence. And in his presence is fullness of joy. This is stated so well in Psalm 16: 11. "You have made known to me the path of my life." NIV.

And if we want peace, Ephesians 2: 14 states that Jesus is our peace. The New Living translation of the Bible puts it this way. "For Christ himself has brought peace to us. He united Jews and Gentiles into one people when, in his own body on the cross, <u>he broke down the wall of hostility that separated us</u>."

Oh how we need the walls of hostility broken down in our nation. But we humans, with our finite abili-

ties, will never succeed without the power of God.
And we will not see the power of God until we open
our hearts to him.

The Psalms Speak to our Hearts

This year, I am reminded of how relevant the Psalms are for life today. They keep cropping up in my devotional. At church, Pastor Dan presented a series called "Summer in the Psalms." Then last week I received notice that "Psalms Alive" is the theme set for the upcoming Java Joy gatherings.

Although I first became familiar with the Psalms when I was a young girl, I still learned a few things from the sermon series and also from a peek at the Java Joy website.

When I was growing up, we lived a mile down the road from Cottonwood Church. From our place, it looked like a white dot on the wheat-covered prairie. Although the church closed many years ago, it has continued to inspire my writing.

Sunday school was a highlight of my week. The family Bible still holds a bookmark that I made for my mother back then. One time we made a dough of salt and flour and fashioned objects from the time of Christ, such as an oil lamp and a bowl. One steamy summer Sunday, we trooped down the outside steps to the basement and tried to hold class there. That ended quickly when we found out that some lizards lived there.

Perhaps my single best experience at Cottonwood Church took place when I was nine. I was surprised to be called to the front of the church during the morning service and presented a black Bible with my name printed on the front in gold; I was graduating to another class!

It was in Sunday school that I learned my way around the Bible. We memorized the books in order and had a new memory verse every week. I still remember, open it in the middle and you are in Psalm 119, and the New Testament begins three quarters of the way through.

Still, it was only as an adult, when I began searching for the meaning of life, that God's message became real to me. Even so, I couldn't particularly relate to the Psalms. Only after I'd been matured by the birth of children, the death of loved ones, and the struggles of life did the Psalms begin speaking to my heart. These 150 songs now console and encourage me. The promises are as trustworthy today as they were when they were written.

When I read through Psalms every year, I find wonders in every chapter. Sometimes it's a special verse, such as when I began my career with a state-wide organization, I underlined Psalm 18: 19: "He also brought me out into a broad place; He delivered me because He delighted in me." Note to readers: He delights in you, also!

Some psalms have been set to today's music. Reading the words may remind me of a song that will then play in my head for the rest of the day. One of those is Psalm 27: 14: "Wait on the Lord, be of good courage, and He shall strengthen your heart; Wait, I say, on the Lord!" That message of waiting isn't one I always want to receive, but it is wisdom to the core.

Sometimes I come upon a verse that I've read many times, but it suddenly makes my heart leap as I see it in a new light. "They shall still bear fruit in old age; They shall be fresh and flourishing." That's

Psalm 92: 14 and it's a promise that I rest in as I sit at the computer every day.

Have you considered reading through the Psalms? Try reading one Psalm a day using a modern language edition, such as the New International Version or the New King James or The Message.

Mint Condition

This post is about my emotional trauma at turning 70 and the resurrection of Grandma Bessie's mint plant. First, the birthday. Sure, I'm grateful to be alive and in relatively good health. At the same time, turning 70 this past summer was tough. It was like falling into a stream, and being unable to fight the current. Keeping up appearances is getting harder all the time.

Age may be a state of mind, but my body doesn't know this. My weight stays about the same, but my body is sagging down, down. All of those funny cards about your boobs resting on your belly? They aren't funny anymore.

Still, if there is a time to embrace your age, it might be 70. A cousin bought a ranch in Montana at age 70 and started over again. My mother worked until she was 73. Remember Miss Lillian, President Carter's mother? She joined the Peace Corps at 75.

My third book, *Amber's Choice,* was published the week I turned 70. Will it be my last book? I don't know, but I'm going to keep writing. Saint Paul encourage his followers to finish the race set before them. I'll stay in the race as long as I can.

Perhaps 70 is the line of demarcation between making a living and living a calling. These years of freedom from work obligations can be like the encore at the end of a concert, or like whipped cream on a dessert.

Now, about that mint. Growing up at LaMoure meant stopping by Grandma Bessie Muir's home at least once a week. I was very familiar with her large yard, and loved the mint that grew against the foundation of her house.

Because my mother owned the property after Bessie died, I acquired a root of the mint when we bought a house in Bismarck. The plant did well. Years later, we moved to another home and transplanted it again. When we moved two years ago, I was dismayed to leave Grandma's mint behind. With four-foot snow drifts in the backyard, there wasn't any way to dig up a plant. I mourned it's loss.

Actually, I whined about it. After all, that mint was older than me, and my book about Grandma Bessie, *Secrets of the Dark Closet*, was about to be published. But that wasn't the end of the mint. The next fall my niece arrived from Minnesota with a root of Grandma's mint plant. Thrilled, I put it in our tiny garden next to the foundation of the house and hoped it would survive winter.

The mint sprang up the next spring and today it's in "mint condition." So far, it's been served in lemonade, gifted to friends, and it helped squelch an invasion of ants. In other words, *it's older than me and still has a purpose.*

Maybe that's because it's always been located close to a foundation that protects it. For we humans, the best foundation we can have is a friendship with Jesus. If we stay close to him, we can trust that he will be with us no matter what. In Matthew 28:20 he even said, "And surely I am with you always, to the very end of the age."

I like the idea of pursuing a calling in my golden years. There are so many needs in the world. Organizations that need volunteers. Friends that need encouragement. Kids that need mentors.

"How wonderful it is that nobody need wait a single moment before starting to improve the world." Anne Frank

From Here to Eternity

Eternity. The word causes fear in some people and hope in others. There is a lot of interest in eternity, judging by the number of books dedicated to the subject. In addition, why wouldn't there be? Doesn't every thinking person want to know what happens when this life is over?

Having grown up attending church and Sunday school, I always vaguely believed in eternal life. As a teen, I remember looking at the moon through the branches of the apple tree in our back yard. I thought that God was kind, but I figured he lived way beyond the moon, out of my reach.

It wasn't until after I was married, when my father's health was declining, that I began a soul-searching look for the truth. I'd sit up late at night, with a bottle of something and my Winston's, and I'd cry and pray.

One midnight I scrawled on a tear-stained sheet of paper the five questions that burned in my soul: Is there really a God? Is there really a heaven? What happens when you die? Why was I born? Why do people suffer?"

In "The Sacred Romance" Brent Curtis and John Eldredge state that, "Our longing for heaven whispers to us in our disappointments and screams at us through our agony." That was what was happening for me. I was in agony over the suffering that my father was going through. I sat up every night talking to God and trying to find answers.

Eventually, I had a turn-the-lightbulb-on moment when I understood that Jesus is the bridge from here to eternity. Realizing that *He lives today* and isn't just a historical figure, helped me find the answers to my questions. How I wish I could have shared that Good News with my dad before he died.

In her devotional *Encouraging Words for Women*, Darlene Sala writes, "We expect too much from this life here on earth. We act as if we can settle down here and make our home here forever. We work and save for retirement, as if it were heaven itself, when in fact 'our citizenship is in heaven' Philippines 3:20. We expect this broken world to hold the answers to peace and happiness."

So, if you haven't thought about what happens to us at the end of life, now is the time. The Bible says much about the afterlife. I've heard people say that they aren't planning to go to heaven because they want to party with their friends in hell. I've got news! The real party is going to take place in heaven.

Teach us to Pray

Would you like to escape to a place where everyone is healthy, happy, and at peace? Yeah, me too. In fact, I've had some good opportunities for that this year. As I wrote *Cottonwood Dreams*, I mentally lived at Cottonwood Creek where life just seems better.

Recently, I've been editing a manuscript for a friend and found myself escaping into her story of a woman who learned how to slip into another world. I began to wish I could push the handle on a water pump and find myself elsewhere.

Actually, there is a way of escape if you're worn out by the pandemic and the political upheaval. You don't need to throw your phone and television in the trash. You don't need to take a trip to another country or time travel to another era.

You can begin with the words of this song by Joe Wise. It speaks to the turmoil that grows in us when we live in a world as agitated as a wringer washer. I hear the song calling me to sit in a quiet room, dwell on each phrase, and examine my own actions and attitudes.

Why and where and when did Mr. Wise write the song? All I know is it's been around since the era of the Viet Nam war, civil rights protests and the sexual revolution. That time was as difficult as what we are going through today, and yet...

Yet, something wonderful came out of that era. Millions of people found new life and hope and faith in God. Some were already church goers, other were

hippies and people who just felt lost and hopeless.
I was among them.

That same renewal can happen today for you and
for me. Please take a moment and read the words
to the song.

Lord, Teach Us to Pray by Joe Wise

Lord, teach us to pray…

It's been a long and cold December kind of day.
With our hearts and hands all busy in our
private little wars.
We stand and watch each other now from
separate shores.
We lose the way.

I need to know today the way things should be
in my head.
I need to know for once now the things that
should be said.
I've got to learn to walk around as if I were not
dead.
I've got to find a way to learn to live. (Refrain)

I still get so distracted by the color of my skin.
I still get so upset now when I find that I don't win.
I meet so many strangers—I'm slow to take them
in.
I've got to find a way to really live. (Refrain)

I stand so safe and sterile as I watch a man fall
flat.
I'm silent with a man who'd like to know just
where I'm at.
With the aged and the lonely I can barely tip my
hat.
I need to see the sin of "I don't care." (Refrain)

I stand so smug and sure before the people I've
out-guessed.
To let a man be who he is I still see as a test.
And when it all comes down to "must," I'm sure
my way is best.
I've got to find what "room" means in my heart.
(Refrain)

Lord, teach us to pray.
We believe that we can find a better way.
Teach us to pray. We lose the way.
Teach us to pray.

I've found that prayer and music are the surest roads to the throne room of God, where there is ample grace and peace for everyone.

About the Author

Gayle Larson Schuck grew up at LaMoure, ND, and has lived in Bismarck for most of her life. She earned a bachelor's degree as an older than average student.

After writing news releases and newsletters for 28 years, she retired to drink her morning coffee on the patio and begin writing books.

Gayle loves to read, garden, spend time with family, and has led Bible studies for many years. All of her books are set in North Dakota. See more at www.gaylelarsonschuck.com.